Chapter 1

Professor Alan Mackilligin spent the last week of his wife's life in their bedroom with her, to be with her at her harrowing end. Her body was so fired with fever that he couldn't share the bed, so he lay on the floor, on her yoga mat. The bed linen had to be changed every four hours, bundled up and collected by the small van from the laundry, which brought it back, ironed, folded, fragrant, the following morning. Marjorie, the woman who came in to clean, stayed with them for the whole of that week, and in those traumatic seven days Mackilligin was tested in everything: his love, faith, patience.

'We need to consider the hospice across in Dundee,' Dr Anderson advised when the GP came downstairs from the bedroom.

'I'd like to try to keep her here,' Mackilligin told the doctor, conscious that it was selfish.

'It may be a question of managing her pain.'

'What if I ask my cousin Andrea to come to stay?' he suggested. 'She's a retired GP in Aberdeenshire.'

'That would certainly give you the cover you need to keep your wife here.'

Andrea moved about silently and professionally, administering the injections of morphine and monitoring Vivien's temperature. He only left their bedroom to have his meals, to go to the toilet and to take a shower. In the first few days Vivien was lucid, and as he lay beside her on the floor she spoke about their first meeting at Edinburgh University, where they had both studied fine art. He confessed that the first time he had seen her, with her face resting on her hand, listening intently to a lecture on the pre-Raphaelites, he had moved up to the same level of tier to admire her, and that by the end of the lecture he knew that he had found his life's partner.

'But you didn't approach me for weeks.'

'That's because I was trying to find the courage.'

'Did I look so formidable?' she asked with a smile.

Vivien and he had their honeymoon on the island of Iona, where her family had a holiday house by a beach and which the Mackilligins had to themselves for a fortnight every August. He read on the hot sands while Vivien swam naked in the secluded bay. She told him that she had first become fascinated by stained glass when she discovered the figure of St Margaret of Scotland in Iona Cathedral, and that as a teenager she had once sat for an hour after her afternoon swim, barefooted as she always was on Iona, gazing up at the window in the clerestory, watching the way the sun lit up the coloured glass as if the saint were about to step out of the frame.

One night in their bedroom in St Andrews she asked him to verify that there was a lump on her left breast. A month before she had been given her most important commission, a window for a church in Fife to replace one blown in, smashed beyond reconstruction in a storm. The centrepiece of the window was the martyred St Andrew lugging his X-shaped cross to his place of execution. Even when she was nauseous with the chemotherapy Vivien

ADORING VENUS

Lorn Macintyre

Best Wishes
Lorn Macintyre

Priormuir Press
St Andrews, Fife

First published in Great Britain in 2011 by
Priormuir Press
St Andrews, Fife KY16 8LP

Phone: 01334 476428
e-mail: priormuirpress@btinternet.com

DISCLAIMER
This is a work of fiction. Any resemblance of characters to
actual persons, living or dead, is purely coincidental.

ISBN 978-0-9567681-1-7

Typeset in St Andrews by Print & Design, University of St Andrews
Printed and bound in Great Britain by Elanders Ltd, North Tyneside

struggled up the stairs to her studio, to cut out the glass to the pattern she had already drawn. But on the night she was told that the malignancy was in her bones, he found her sobbing as she tried with trembling fingers to piece together the image of the crucified saint, the cross crooked.

He tried to prepare himself for her death when he accepted that there was no hope, but without her seeing his despair. But he knew that he couldn't begin the grieving process early and that only through her passing would come the full realization of his loss.

The last week was both hellish and inspiring. She was too hot, too frail to take in his arms, and he could see that she wanted release.

'Will I increase the dose of morphine?' his medical cousin whispered to him when he came downstairs.

He knew what she meant. The thought of parting from Vivien was unbearable, but he acquiesced and she was cold by midnight.

He had always been moderate in his consumption of alcohol, but in bereavement found that he needed the support of drink because of the violence of the conflicting emotions, celebrating her exemplary life and exceptional talent, lamenting the cruelty of her death, as if his being were pouring out through his tear ducts, which was why he had resorted to the bottle, and why his cousin had to put him to bed in the spare room. Vivien and he had discussed her funeral arrangements. She had repaired a stained glass window in a small church in the East Neuk, and that was where she wanted to be buried after a Christian service.

They had gone to see the graveyard when he brought her home from her final hopeless consultation in Dundee. It was a June evening, warm, with bees murmurous in the aromatic shrubberies, and he could see why she had chosen its peace, but he also saw the terror in her face as he helped her, weakened by chemotherapy, round her resting place.

But when it came to actually lowering her into that ground in the narrow polished box, he broke down. During that last week in the bedroom with her he had begun to experience the terror of being left alone, after so many years with a loving and loved companion with whom he had shared so much. They had been students together in the libertine 1960s, but hadn't slept together until their marriage, because his respect for her had amounted to idealization. With her gone it was unbearable.

They had been so pleased to have been able to buy the early nineteenth century house in a street near the castle. It had an outside stone staircase because the property had originally been two separate fisherfolks' cottages, and there was a calotype by Hill and Adamson, the pioneers of photography, of women sitting on the staircase, mending nets.

At the back of the house a set of steps led up from the pleasant lounge to a small walled garden which Vivien completely replanted. He would come home from university to see her shapely rump on the lawn above as she pressed another bulb into the soil. They both loved that house of light, the white staircase up to the bedrooms with their coomed ceilings, the bathroom in which he had painstakingly stripped the wall lining back to the original pine. One of the bedrooms had been turned into her studio, and they had installed a roof-light above her work table.

On winter nights the wind from the nearby sea funnelled up the narrow street, making them feel secure as they lay in bed behind the closed shutters he had freed from many coats of paint. On summer evenings, when they took their supper plates out to the garden, it was so quiet, as if they were in a remote village, not one of the most popular holiday resorts in Scotland. After Vivien's death he didn't want to go home to a house that seemed cold and alien, as if they had never occupied it. He hadn't found solace in alcohol on the night she had died, and he avoided it. He tried to work in his office, but instead of studying slides of statues on the light-box, he sat remembering their years together. He tried to cook for himself, but even the everyday utensils in the kitchen evoked memories of the meals they had had together with candles and wine, and he would find himself weeping as he stirred the soup, his tears hissing on the blue ring of burning gas.

He was in bad shape. Dr Anderson stopped him in the street and, having commented that he had lost weight, asked how he was coping. When he shook his head the doctor urged him to come to see him at the surgery. 'I'll give you something to help you over this harrowing time.'

But he didn't want tranquillizers or sleeping pills, because he knew that his grief was an expression of his intense love for his late wife and that he had to learn to live with the loss. He had always been a sound sleeper, but found himself waking in the dawn and switching on the radio. The news bulletins were filled with violence and death in Iraq and Afghanistan: a woman carrying a wicker cage containing two doves into a crowded Baghdad market, detonating the explosives the birds were sitting on. Yet another British soldier blown up in Helmand Province.

Should he be crying for someone who had lived a full and happy life for sixty one years, when the news bulletins were reporting children murdered and maimed in conflicts? These were the questions he asked himself, but they were always answered by more outpourings of grief. One night he tipped Vivien's lingerie drawer onto their bed and buried his distraught face in garments still fragrant from the lavender sachets she had placed among them.

The garden was being neglected, the grass too long, the flowerbeds invaded by weeds when she had kept it so neat and ordered. He should bring in a person to maintain it, but that seemed like an intrusion. At least the house was clean and tidy, because Marjorie was coming in two mornings a week now.

He was invited out to supper by a friend in History. There were two other couples present, and the conversation turned to his recent bereavement.

'We lost our daughter to leukaemia three years ago,' one of the women disclosed. 'I wouldn't have been able to cope if it weren't for the medium I consulted.'

At first he thought the guest at the table was one of the New Age types he had come to distrust through seeing them on Iona, camping on the western machair, hoping to be put in touch with the spirit of St Columba through a combination of cannabis and meditation. But the woman was evidently sincere, and on an impulse he asked her for the address of the medium. The following week he took a train to Edinburgh, and a taxi to the address in the New Town. The woman who answered the door was dressed in a kimono. She led him across the sanded boards of a drawing-room perfumed by a candle, to a high-backed chair where she asked him to relax as she held both his hands.

'Please don't tell me anything about yourself,' she had requested on the phone.

'Your wife is in spirit,' she announced after a few minutes of concentration.

'Yes she is,' he confirmed, though she could have read this from his demeanour.

'Your wife was very artistic.'

He waited to be told what her artistic interest was.

'She was a very capable woman.'

'In what way?' he challenged the medium.

'She was very particular about how the house looked.'

But many women are house-proud.

'Your wife is in the spirit world with her mother.'

'What was her mother's name?' he tested her.

The medium appeared to be having a conversation with someone, because she kept nodding her head.

'I can't quite make out what's being said.'

'To whom are you speaking?' he wanted to know.

'My spirit guide. She's relaying messages from your wife. That's the way it works in the spirit world. I'm sorry, I can't get the name, but I'm being told that your wife was in great pain before she died.'

But that could be an inspired guess.

'She wants you to know that she's happy where she is, and looking forward to being reunited with you in the fullness of time.'

He paid the forty pounds and went back to St Andrews, more angry than disappointed, feeling that he had been exploited. When the woman who had suggested the appointment phoned him to find out how it had gone, he told her that he thought the medium was a fraud, taking money by false pretences.

'I don't agree,' she said indignantly. 'She gave us very good evidence about the survival of our daughter.'

The experience with the medium made his depression even deeper. It was the summer vacation, and he wondered if it wouldn't be advisable to take a holiday – perhaps abroad. Vivien and he had been to Greece and Italy several times, and were particularly fond of Rome, where they spent most of the time looking at the stained glass in churches. But the thought of going abroad without her was too much to bear.

He tried to submerge his grieving by going into his office every day. A new intake of students would arrive in September, but going through their records only took a couple of days. He tried to return to his research, a book on Hellenistic sculpture, but found that he couldn't concentrate. Somehow he got through that summer, and when the students came in late September he had plenty to keep himself occupied, with interviews and meetings. He didn't get home until late, and that made it easier, because having heated a supermarket meal from the freezer for supper, he went to bed and slept soundly. He was tired, and began to wonder again if he should retire. But to where? Could he bear to stay alone in the St Andrews house, rising in the morning with no fixed responsibilities? Wouldn't he be even more depressed, with life becoming more and more aimless? Even if he resumed his book on Hellenistic sculpture, that would only take a year to complete, and what then?

Every evening on his way up to bed, turning into Vivien's studio and standing by her work-table had become a ritual. He touched the uncompleted stained glass window as if somehow he could summon its creator back to life. The blue fragments of glass reminded him of the sea around Iona, and so many memories came flooding back that he found himself sitting with his head in his hands on the stairs. Perhaps he needed to get rid of the uncompleted window, if he were to feel happy again. Perhaps he needed to put Vivien's clothes – still in the wardrobes and drawers – into the car and take them round to a charity shop. But he couldn't bring himself to dispose of the stained glass and the clothes because it seemed a rejection of her.

He dreaded putting the key into the lock, opening the door into a deserted house. Sitting on the bed in which his wife had suffered and died, he hugged her slippers to his heart, howling at her loss for which nothing could compensate, not even his scholarship.

On this particular September evening he was crossing

the quad of St Salvator's College when he heard the organ being played in the Chapel. He entered the cloisters and pulled open the heavy wooden door with the authentic iron latch, walking down the flagstoned aisle to the tier of high-backed pews on the left where he had sat when he and Vivien had attended Chapel regularly when they had first come to St Andrews. He had been enchanted by the ritual of putting on his academic robes in the Hebdomadar's Room and lining up with the other professors and lecturers behind the Principal, the bedellus leading the way, carrying in his white-gloved fist one of the university maces, with the silver figure of St Andrew on top. Mackilligin had done one of the readings, raising his eyes from the Bible to see Vivien nodding to him, signalling that he had done well. But he had stopped attending chapel when the novelty wore off.

Sixteen years later he was back, sitting by himself in the front pew, opposite the Playfair stained glass window, the burning bush of Moses extinguished as the day faded as he listened to the organ recital. It was Bach, and he had sufficient of an ear to know that the player was highly skilled. The music seemed to roll over him, a cleansing tide taking with it his grief. When the cantata was over he applauded, and a figure appeared at the railing of the organ loft and bowed to him. It was a young woman, but her features weren't distinct in the evening light through the long stained glass windows which seemed to lay little fires on the marble floor.

The player disappeared and the organ started up again. Unknown to the listener the musician was watching him in the small screen of the monitor beside her, connected to the camera pointing down the aisle to the altar to co-ordinate the music for the weddings of alumni held in the Chapel. When the organ went silent he applauded again, and as he was rising to leave the player came down the aisle on swift silent feet.

'I didn't realise I had an audience.'

'It was wonderful. I could sit listening to you all evening.'

She reminded him of Vivien with her attractive features framed by long dark hair that reached beyond her shoulders. Most of the students dressed in T-shirts and denims, but she was wearing a blue knee-length dress beneath her red gown.

'Where did you learn to play like that?'

'My father taught me. He's the organist at our church. He started me at nine, when my feet could just reach to the pedals. I played for my first wedding when I was twelve.'

'Where do you come from?' he asked, trying to place her accent.

'Edinburgh.'

'What are you studying?'

'Classics and theology.'

'What year are you in?'

'This is my first year.'

'And you like it?'

'I love St Andrews.'

'Where are you staying?'

'McIntosh Hall. Are you connected with the university?'

'I'm a professor in art history. Alan Mackilligin,' he said, holding out his hand.

'I'm Rebecca Campbell-Arthurson. Next to music art was my favourite subject at school.'

'Couldn't you have taken an art option with classics and theology?' he asked.

'I never thought of that.'

'You could still change, it's so early in the term.'

'I think I'd better stick with classics and theology.'

What else could he ask her to detain her, because he was grateful for her company and didn't want to go home? But a porter came in to say that he was locking up, and Mackilligin followed her out. As they stood in the cloisters he wondered if he should ask her to his house for a coffee, but by the time he had found the courage she had said goodnight and disappeared. He poured himself a whisky and went to sit in the back garden among its neglected borders, pondering that the image of the organ player of sacred music was one of innocence which the great painters of the past would have illuminated.

She was a teenage student and he a sixty one year old professor. Why would she be interested in keeping his company when there were so many students of her own age on the campus? He went indoors for a second whisky, returning to sit in the twilight of the hushed town where he had experienced so much happiness in his personal life and fulfilment as an art historian. The warmth of the whisky seemed to enhance the image of the organ player at the railing of the loft. He hadn't felt so relaxed since before his wife's illness, and when he put the whisky glass into the sink it was the first night that he didn't go into her studio on his way up to bed.

When he had undressed he stood in front of the pier-glass that Vivien had bought in an antique shop and studied his body. The muscles he had built up through punishing games of squash throughout his forties and fifties had gone flabby, but there were only a few broken veins like small blue sprigs on his calves, whereas the feet of a friend in Physics, with whom he swam once a week, looked as if they had been painted with gentian violet. He needed to get back into shape and would rejoin the squash ladder, though he had seen another friend, a chemist, gripping the little black ball as he lay gasping against the wall, expiring through cardiac arrest before the ambulance arrived with the defibrillator.

He remembered how, as a child after listening to the band in the Glasgow park, he had fallen asleep with bagpipes still ringing in his ears. That night in his bed in St Andrews he drifted away to Bach on the St Salvator's organ.

Chapter 2

The following evening Mackilligin went back to the Chapel, but it was locked, and there was no sound of the organ. He was disconsolate as he walked home. Perhaps the student only practised once a week. Perhaps she was avoiding him because he had asked her too many questions. That night he sat with the cap off the whisky bottle before stumbling on the stairs on the way up to bed, pausing on the landing, his hand on the door handle of his wife's studio. He hesitated, then opened the door. The incomplete stained glass window laid out on the table angered him. There was no God, no afterlife in which to meet the beloved departed. He lurched into the room and swept the pieces to the floor. The act seemed to sober him up, and he went down on his knees, scooping the coloured shards up into his palms, his hands bleeding from the sharp edges as he dropped them back on to the table. Through his tears he tried to reassemble the jigsaw of the window, but he couldn't remember where the pieces went, and besides, St Andrew's cross had been shattered in the fall to the floor.

He sat on the floor, sobbing as he asked forgiveness from his wife for this sacrilege.

'It isn't that I don't love you; I'm lonely. I'm losing my faith and I don't know what to believe in any more. What should I do? Retire and sell up? But to where? I don't know what got into me, doing this to your work. I should have kept it as a memorial to you, commissioned someone else to finish it to your design. I'm like this because I'm very lonely. Forgive me, darling. It's hard.'

When he went into his office next morning with a heavy head an internal e-mail awaited him.

> *I have a 1st year classics and theology student who would like to sit in on your lectures on female beauty portrayed in classical sculpture when they don't clash with her other lectures. Agreeable?*

He typed back immediately: *Of course. Regards, Alan.*

Instead of going home to heat a can of soup at lunchtime he went to an Indian restaurant in College Street and enjoyed an appetising meal for the first time since his wife's passing. He felt younger, invigorated, still capable of being surprised by life. When he went home after conducting a very successful seminar he found that Marjorie had been, and that the house was spotless. Vivien had always done the garden, except the grass, and he didn't have enough skill to weed the beds without damaging the plants, so he used Yellow Pages to find a company that would come in and restore it.

That evening he didn't go round to the Chapel in the hope that Rebecca was playing the organ. He was content to wait until she turned up at a lecture. And he didn't have a nightcap. Instead he climbed to bed, without going into the studio and slept soundly. He had a lengthy bath instead of a shower the next morning and went in early to work. He was bending over his light-box, selecting slides of statues for his lectures when someone spoke behind him, and he turned to see Rebecca.

'The door was open.'

'You're very welcome,' he told her, opening his arms as if he were going to embrace her.

'I don't have any lectures this morning, so I thought I'd come.'

He had always been at ease when dealing with students, but had never been in a close relationship with one. Children of his own would have given him skills with the young.

'What did I miss yesterday?' she asked.

'I gave the students an introductory talk. I start my lectures on beauty in classical sculpture this morning.'

Mackilligin began his series of lectures by making a distinction between the Hellenic and Hellenistic period of Greek history and of sculpture. 'The Hellenic period, dated between approximately 900 and 323 BC., refers to the era of the rise of the Greek city-states such as Athens and Sparta. The Hellenistic period – which is my period of study – is taken to be the era from the death of Alexander the Great in 323 BC to the middle of the First Century BC. It was characterised by Greek and Macedonian emigration to areas conquered by Alexander, and also by the spread of Greek civilization from Greece to Northern India.'

Mackilligin projected an image on the screen. 'This statue comes from the Hellenic period. One reason for beginning my lecture series in this period and with this statue is because it's the first life-size representation of the nude female form in classical sculpture. It's known as the Colonna Venus. It's a Roman marble copy of the lost Aphrodite of Cnidus by Praxiteles. The version we're looking at is the best-known and perhaps most faithful Roman copy of the most renowned sculpture of antiquity. Aphrodite, the Roman Venus, goddess of love and beauty, was born out of the foam of the sea.

'Pliny says of this statue: "...and yet superior to anything not merely by Praxiteles, but in the whole world, is the Venus." In the *Amores,* attributed to Lucian, the statue is described in these words:

> ...we entered the temple. In the midst thereof sits the goddess – she is a most beautiful statue of Parian marble - arrogantly smiling a little as a grin parts her lips. Draped by no garment, all her beauty is uncovered and revealed, except in so far as she unobtrusively uses one hand to hide her private parts. So great was the power of the craftsman's art that the hard unyielding marble did justice to every limb... The temple had a door on both sides for the benefit of those also who wish to have a good view of the goddess from behind, so that no part of her be left unadmired. It's easy therefore for people to enter by the other door and survey the beauty of her back. And so we decided to see all of the goddess and went round to the back of the precinct. Then, when the door had been opened by the woman responsible for keeping the keys, we were filled with an immediate wonder for the beauty we beheld.'

Mackilligin continued: 'There's a paradox here. The goddess Aphrodite hated to be seen naked by mortals – unless she herself initiated the encounter. If she caught voyeurs, they were dealt with mercilessly. So was Lucian, and are we, voyeurs as we look upon her, albeit in marble? Praxiteles would have been aware of the paradox when he fashioned her. Is she goddess or desirable woman?

'The Greek philosopher Plato made a distinction between two types of Venus in his *Symposium*: *Venus Coelestis* and *Venus Naturalis*, Celestial Venus and Vulgar Venus. Praxiteles's Aphrodite is a *Venus Coelestis*, and is a type of statue also known as *Venus Pudica*, Modest Venus.

'She's preparing for a ritual bath to restore her purity, or she's had her bath, and is discarding her drapery in her left hand over a water jar. The right hand is covering her private parts, though her pubic hair and vulva have been omitted. This is in striking contrast to the representation of genitals on male bodies in Greek sculpture. Did the Greeks consider that female genitals on statues would have been viewed as immodest?

'Does this statue of Aphrodite by Praxiteles represent sexual temptation, or the chaste veneration of the body beautiful? After all, he's portraying a goddess who would render a man impotent for life if he dared look upon her naked without invitation. It has been argued that a timeless Platonic ideal is embodied in this statue's transcendent beauty. Greek sculptors sought to portray the ideal human figure. Plato believed that in sculpture, as in all things in life, there exists a perfect form which embodies beauty and good. I suggest that in the Aphrodite of Cnidus we venerate her beauty and see in it spiritual and not sexual attractions. She is to be worshipped, not lusted after.'

Next Mackilligin projected an image of the statue of

the Venus de Milo on to the screen. 'She's named after the Greek island of Melos, where she was discovered in 1820 in a buried niche by a peasant. The statue has been dated to around 100BC in the Hellenistic period. Her arms are missing, though that doesn't seem to detract from the perfection of her beauty. But close study of the statue suggests that the right arm of the goddess was lowered across the torso, with the hand resting on the raised left knee so that the drapery, which seems to be sliding down her hips could be held in place, a potent image of modesty. Part of the evidence for the disposition of the right arm comes from the filled cavity below the right breast which originally contained a metal tenon that would have supported the separately carved right arm.

'What about the left arm, which is entirely amputated? The sculpture was found on Melos with fragments of a left hand holding an apple. Close examination suggests that the left arm was held below the eye level of the statue above a square stone pillar, while holding an apple. The goddess would have been gazing at the apple. Do we take this as a symbol of temptation, forbidden fruit? In ancient Greek Melos means apple. But the apple that Venus – let's call her Aphrodite – is assumed to have been holding probably refers to Aphrodite's victory in the Judgement of Paris when Paris awarded her the golden apple in return for the love of the most beautiful woman in the world, Helen of Sparta, wife of the Greek king Menelaus, which caused the Trojan War, which is perhaps a warning about how love – or desire – can be destructive.

'Does the apple the Venus de Milo had in her left hand also relate to the story from Genesis of Eve and her apple? Both the Jews and the Greeks wrote about apples that were a cause of strife, and the Hebrew Bible was translated by the Greeks. It's an intriguing thought, except that the Bible does not actually state that the forbidden fruit was an apple.

'In its intact state this statue of Venus would have been tinted and adorned with jewellery to make it appear lifelike. We know about these adornments because the attachment holes can be located. This lady is a survivor. France purchased the statue from the Melos peasant, and it was eventually presented to the Louvre in Paris. In the autumn of 1939, with war expected, Venus was crated and removed to a safe refuge in the French countryside, which is why we are able to admire her today. Some critics have seen the drapery slipping down her thighs as a sexual symbol, but I believe that she's stopping it slipping through modesty.'

At the end of the lecture Rebecca complimented him on how 'enlightening' it had been.

'You made me want to go Paris to see the statue.'

'Maybe one day you'll make a visit to the Louvre. Would you like some lunch?'

'Thanks, but I've arranged to meet someone.'

He knew that it was unworthy, but he felt despondent at the thought of her meeting another student, when he could have had her company. He had a tutorial that afternoon, but he was unusually silent and knew from the faces of the students that they hadn't got much out of it.

He went home at six, making himself an omelette. His

depression was returning. He left his supper unfinished and went out for a walk. He arrived at the Chapel, but it was locked and in silence. He didn't want to go home and instead sat with a coffee and a pastry in a coffee shop which was throbbing with music, the sofas crowded with students talking loudly, some of them working on laptops. He was becoming conscious of his age, uncomfortable at the thought that he was the oldest person in the coffee house. But he also knew that no one around him was paying any attention to him, as if he didn't exist.

He knew that he had lost his sense of purpose in life. His marriage had been the perfect relationship because, as he was researching his book on Hellenistic sculpture in the university library, Vivien would be working at her stained glass window, the spotlights beamed on the glass she was cutting with such care and precision. He had lost his wife but needed to get back to his vocation. On his way home from the noisy coffee house he went into the university library and up to the art section on the top floor. He took a book into a carrel, but found that he couldn't focus on the Hellenistic statues.

Rebecca was sitting in the front row of his lecture the following morning, and afterwards she came up to him, to thank him and to tell him how much she had learnt.

'Why don't we go down to Edinburgh on Saturday? I want to show you a statue in the National Galleries.'

'I'd like that,' his new student said eagerly.

He arranged that he would drive them to Leuchars and take the train. They sat shoulder to shoulder and talked about art and his love of Iona.

'Have you ever been there? Then you must go,' he urged her. 'It has this unique atmosphere. The island actually divides into two parts. There's the eastern part where the abbey is and where St Columba's monastery of wood and wattle was. It's very beautiful, with its bays of white sands and blue waters. You can feel the sanctity of this part of the island, as if the stones and crosses have absorbed it. Then there's the western part. It's unpopulated and rugged, and has a rather sinister reputation among certain of the islanders and some of the visitors, as if there are elemental forces lurking there.'

'Elemental forces?' his travelling companion queried.

'I'm not sure that I understand the phrase myself,' he said lightly as the autumnal woods of Fife disappeared backwards, as if they were being felled. 'An Italian woman is buried among the kings of Scotland in the graveyard. I was told that she went to the island in the 1920s to try to communicate with elemental forces. She went missing one night and was found naked, with a cross cut out on the turf beside her, and with a knife in her fist, as if she'd been defending herself in some occult ritual.'

'An encounter with the Devil?' Rebecca suggested.

'Maybe she was trying to slay Satan, who knows?'

'Do you believe in the Devil?' she asked.

He was taken aback by the question, but realised that he had to be cautious in his answer, since this was a theology student.

'I don't believe in him as a figure – as opposed to an angel

– with horns and a forked tail as has been portrayed in art down the centuries. But I certainly believe that there are evil forces, on a global as well as a personal level. We have the extermination policies of the Nazis and serial killers such as the Moors Murderers. And there are lower grades of evil.'

'I've an essay to write on the differences between evil and immorality.'

'That's a very big question for a first term assignment,' he conceded. 'If I were a philosopher I could help you, but I'm an art historian. Certainly there are deeds thought to be evil portrayed in paintings, such as the severance of John the Baptist's head, and Courbet was accused of immorality for painting *L'Origine du monde*, showing a woman's spread thighs and genitals. But you're answering the question about life, not art, and even if we were sitting on a train to London, we wouldn't finish a discussion on that topic before we reached the capital.'

They walked along Princes Street to the National Galleries, where he led her to the sculpture of The Three Graces.

'You might think that this is a statue from classical times, and certainly in the Louvre in Paris there's a Roman copy of a Greek Hellenistic statue of the Three Graces dated to the second century BC and restored in the Renaissance by Nicolas Cordier. The Three Graces, Euphrosyne, Aglaia and Thalia, were the daughters of Zeus and were said to represent beauty, charm and joy. They presided over banquets to entertain and delight the guests. But this group, with arms linked as in the Louvre statue, was actually sculpted early in the nineteenth century by an Italian, Antonio Canova. The story of how this sculpture came into existence is interesting. The 6th Duke of Bedford visited Canova in his studio in Rome, and was enchanted by a carving of the Three Graces which the sculptor had executed for the Empress Josephine of France. When she died in the same year Bedford tried to buy the completed piece, but the Empress's son claimed it, so the Duke commissioned another version – this one – for himself.

'No wonder that the statue took three years to complete, when it was carved from a single block of white marble. The sculptor had assistants who hacked out a rough version of the three figures, and Canova finished it. They're nude, but their lower bodies are partially draped by the scarf which links them. What do you think of them?'

'They look happy in their huddle,' Rebecca observed.

'Sharing a secret or a joke, perhaps. He's portraying them as nubile young women, but at the same time their poise suggests modesty and chastity, does it not?'

He proposed lunch in the restaurant attached to the Galleries, and took the tray out onto the large sun terrace in the balmy autumnal day, with people at adjacent tables sitting with bare arms. He was about to go for more coffee when she said: 'My parents would like to meet you.'

He stopped on his way to the counter. What did this mean? How would her parents view one of her professors taking their daughter to Edinburgh?

'That would be nice,' he said meekly. 'When are we to go?'

'I said around three.'

'Today?'

'Yes, I told them I was coming to Edinburgh with you to the Galleries and they said that they would like to meet you.'

He went for more coffee, since they still had an hour to spend.

'What will you do when you graduate?' he asked.

'I hope to teach.'

'Classics?' he asked, surprised. 'I thought they'd practically disappeared from the school curriculum.'

'They're actually making a comeback – especially in private schools. I'd like to combine classics with religious instruction.'

'I'm surprised that religion's taught in schools, considering the number of nationalities we have in Scotland now.'

'There are still classes, not specifically teaching Christianity, because of course you can have Muslims and other faiths. It's a challenge.'

'You have strong beliefs yourself?' he asked the attractive young woman sitting beneath the backdrop of the castle.

'I'm a practising Catholic.'

Chapter 3

The trouble with developing an obsession with classical sculpture, Mackilligin acknowledged to himself, was that it had made him old before his time and had caused him to miss out on the vibrant 1960s. He had gone to Edinburgh University in 1964, and one of his lecturers, long-haired and in a kaftan, had expressed incredulity that one of his students should prefer the classical statue of Venus de Milo to the same subject sculpted by Niki de Saint Phalle in 1961 from plaster of Paris on chicken wire, with plastic bags full of red and black paint inside it. She had fired a gun at it, broaching the bags, so that the paint seeped through the white plaster, creating a bleeding effect. 'Brilliant,' the lecturer, a cannabis aficionado, had enthused.

Though there were juke-boxes in some of the student cafés Mackilligin frequented with his new-found love Vivien, he wasn't appreciative of the Beatles and the deafening hyperactivity of The Stones. He preferred *Eine Kleine Nachtmusik*. During the Summer of Love, when beauties in diaphanous dresses were walking bare-footed in Hyde Park, flowers behind their ears, Mackilligin, still a virgin, like his sweetheart, was on his first visit to Iona, invited to Vivien's family's holiday home.

They had been very happy and fulfilled in St Andrews, where he had been appointed a professor, having been a lecturer in Edinburgh University. In St Andrews he became even more of a traditionalist, taking to wearing a waistcoat and going to lectures on the history of the town. He didn't find sitting on the Senate boring, because this was where important decisions about the future of the university he cared so much for were made. They spent their annual August holiday on Iona where Vivien worked at small-scale stained glass in the bedroom she had turned into a studio. They walked, watched birds, lived on shellfish, love-making and creative expression and slept exhausted.

Now in his early sixties and still wearing a tie, when the majority of the academic community had shed theirs, and wearing creased trousers when denims were seen at the Senate, the art historian was sitting in a taxi beside a student less than a third of his age, on his way to meet her parents. How was he going to be introduced?

'This is Professor Mackilligin, who has very kindly let me sit in on his course on classical sculpture. We've been looking at the statue of The Three Graces in the National Galleries.'

He shook hands with the petite woman who opened the door of the villa in Morningside in response to the resonant bell, introducing herself as Felicity Campbell-Arthurson. She was dressed in a pastel-coloured knitted woollen suit. He followed her high heels which were banded in gold past an oval table on which a hat, a walking stick and a dog lead were laid. There was a foot-high crucifix on the wall of the hall, and in a recess a grandfather clock with a burnished face was ticking, its brass-weighted intestines showing through the engraved glass door. Mackilligin was now crossing mellow boards into a well-proportioned drawing-room, its bay window overlooking a lawn. He could smell the polish of his childhood.

'My husband's at rugby.'

Rebecca explained that her father, a classics master at a private school in Edinburgh, was refereeing a match between Fettes and Loretto. That explained the silver trophy of a speeding rugby player with a ball under his arm on the mantelpiece, beside invitation cards propped against the gilded mirror, and a wooden statuette of Mary with Child. The visitor was invited to sit down on the sofa which faced two arm-chairs, with lace antimacassars. He surmised that the rosewood bureau, open, with a letter on the tooled leather flap, must be a family heirloom.

As the hostess lifted off a cloth to reveal afternoon tea Mackilligin recognised the classic Spode pattern. The scones had been halved and buttered, the fruit cake cut.

'Milk and sugar, professor?'

It was a deferential address and, as he spread the linen napkin on his knee, the guest began to feel uncomfortable, though not through the position of his spine. The strain was on his nerves. What was this woman, whose alert face he was watching beyond the fragrant stream from the spout, thinking?

'It's very kind of you to give of your valuable time taking Rebecca to the Galleries.'

Mackilligin placed her in her late forties. Was the deference for his age or his academic title? He found it strange and sometimes disconcerting, as he grew older, that he addressed people as though they were of the same generation as himself, whereas they could be twenty, thirty years younger.

'I'm very glad that Rebecca has decided to sit in on my lectures,' he told her mother.

'You were very interested in art when you were at school, weren't you?' she turned to her daughter.

Mackilligin found that he was relaxing in the company of the two women. Her husband arrived half an hour later, a handsome man with close-cut grey hair, wearing a track-suit with a whistle on a lanyard round his neck. As he introduced himself as Diarmid the visitor saw in his face a strength which wasn't likely to be challenged on the rugby pitch when he called a penalty kick. In the referee's whole demeanour, in the way that he relaxed into the chair as his wife served him tea, Mackilligin was observing a life of privilege, teaching in a private school where there were no disciplinary problems and where the majority of the pupils were motivated. His classes were small, so he could get good results, sending pupils to Oxford and Cambridge. He was a person full of confidence in his own abilities and opinions, and this made Mackilligin uneasy, because, if he saw the slightest sign that the guest was emotionally interested in his daughter, he would stop the relationship.

'I read classics at St Andrews,' the referee surprised him by revealing.

'And you were happy there?'

'Very happy. I played cricket, tennis and rugby, and every morning before breakfast I went for a run along the West Sands. How long have you been teaching at St Andrews, professor?'

'Sixteen years.'

'That was after my time. And you like it?'

'I'm very contented there.'

'Rebecca told us that you lost your wife earlier this year. We're so sorry,' her mother sympathised.

'Thank you. It's been difficult, but I'm coping by immersing myself in work.'

'You could stay here for the night,' his hostess offered.

He declined politely, saying that he had to get back to St Andrews.

'You must come again,' she invited him, and her husband concurred.

Mackilligin wanted to phone a taxi, but the classics master insisted on driving them to the station. The art historian sat in the back as father and daughter chatted. The sportsman's hand grip was almost painful in its firmness as they parted at the station.

'Your parents are very hospitable,' he remarked when they were seated on the train.

'They like you.'

They pulled away from the city, the railway sidings now supporting smart flats, claustrophobic in their proximity, as if they had been built for voyeurs. As the train rumbled over the Forth Bridge, into Fife, their conversation faltered. Rebecca was looking down on the grey water between the flickering lattices of the bridge's stanchions.

'You're very lucky having such parents.'

She didn't reply, continuing to gaze out of the window.

'You said your wife was an artist,' she spoke after ten

minutes or so.

'A stained glass artist – a very gifted one. She was never short of commissions. In fact she was working on a major one when she died of cancer. It was all very quick and cruel.'

'Do you have a family?'

'No children – unfortunately.'

'I wish I had a brother or sister,' she said wistfully.

'I wasn't an only child myself, but it must be lonely at times, being by oneself. But you must have made friends at school?'

'Not really. The other girls didn't have the same interests as me. They were into pop music. They didn't want conversations; when they weren't in class their ears were plugged, listening to tunes they'd downloaded, or else they were talking to boyfriends on their mobile phones.'

'You don't like pop music?' he prompted.

'My parents don't like me listening to it. They say that it'll damage my musical ear. I've had violin, piano and organ lessons.'

'Which is your favourite instrument?' he asked.

'The organ. It's got such a majestic sound. You're sitting there, using your hands and feet, and you get the impression that you're controlling a whole orchestra. I love playing sacred music – especially William Byrd. Do you know Byrd's pieces?'

'The name's familiar, but I can't say I'm closely acquainted with his music,' he admitted. 'I can appreciate good music, but I never learned to play an instrument. I regret that now.'

'But you're talented in other ways. You know so much

about classical sculpture. I love your lectures and wish I'd taken art history instead of classics, but my father would never allow me to change.'

'It's your life,' he reminded her.

'But they're supporting me at university.'

He sensed that she wanted to talk more about her relationship with her parents, but that something was holding her back. He didn't question her on the topic, and they lapsed into silence for the rest of the journey. He drove her back to her Hall in time for supper. When he entered his lonely house, which seemed even lonelier that evening, he didn't cook. He had wanted to sit and chat with her because he was happy and restful in her company.

Perhaps what he needed to do was to switch on his laptop and start searching for a site offering to bring the mature lonely together in a relationship. What was he to post? *Academic, aged 61, still trim, with interest in Hellenistic sculpture, wishes to find like-minded female.* Oh Christ, it sounded so sad. No, he was better on his own. Instead of looking for an internet date, he should boot up the laptop and immerse himself in the book he was writing. 'When will you finish your book?' Vivien had asked him with the last of her strength on that last traumatic week with her, and he had promised to work on it.

That evening, prompted by these memories, and with tears in his eyes, he drove out to the East Neuk cemetery which she had chosen. It was an appealing peaceful place in the last of the light, but his heart wasn't lifted as he raised the latch on the black painted gate. Her grave was against the wall where creepers had found a grip in the gaps between the stones. Rooks were cawing in the trees overhead as he stood at the oblong of earth that looked like an ancient tumulus, but it was only months old, and the handles on the coffin beneath the uneven unknitted turf wouldn't even have tarnished. When he raised his eyes from his partner's grave he saw in the wall of the church the stained glass window she had designed on the theme of the text *Come all ye that labour and are heavy laden and I will give you rest.* She had depicted Christ raising His hands in blessing.

He felt angry, not at his late wife's design, but at the untruth of the assertion. Years before, sitting on a beach on Iona, Vivien and he had talked about death, because on that white strand monks had been martyred by the Vikings.

'Let's make a pact. Whoever dies first will try to make contact,' she had urged him.

He didn't want such a sombre conversation on such a beautiful day, especially when they were only in their forties, both healthy, their bare limbs tanned.

'You won't go before me,' she predicted earnestly.

Since her death he hadn't felt her presence in their house, and he hadn't noticed anything moved as a sign that she had come back. As he stood by her grave he didn't sense that she had survived death. The disturbed ground beyond his shoes was where everything had ended, leaving him only with memories and photographs. During the many summers they had spent on Iona they had attended services in the cathedral, and when she climbed the mound to

Columba's cell in front of the cathedral, where the saint had slept with a stone for a pillar, Vivien had reported a feeling of peace and insight. She was into alternative energies, and on fine mornings she would practise Tai-Chi in their garden at St Andrews, as if she were passing an invisible ball between her hands. She was sure that there was another life to come, and that it would be more revealing and more fulfilling than this one.

He didn't believe this as he stood at her graveside. Death was the end; those who hoped otherwise were duped. It was a belief born out of anxiety and, ultimately, terror at the process of growing old, the hope that there has to be something beyond this life, since human beings have been given such powerful emotions, such appreciation of beauty. An agnostic before her death, the widower had now become an atheist, but didn't feel that it was a betrayal of his wife as he turned his back on her grave. Why put up a stone with fancy lettering, when, in twenty years, it would be illegible? Surely the stained glass window in the wall of the church beyond the grave was her memorial, her name on it in small writing beside Christ's bare left foot.

As he dropped the latch on the gate he didn't think that he would go back to the cemetery, despite its tranquillity. That didn't mean that he loved his wife less, he told himself as he backed the car out of the park and headed towards St Andrews. He had to take a large whisky before he could sleep, and even then he was up to the toilet in the middle of the night, when the house felt cold and hostile, the shadow cast by the bathroom light across the passage and against the door of his wife's studio sinister looking. He wondered if he should move, because the associations of the house were beginning to unnerve him. But he knew that it would be a bad idea because, even if he bought all new furniture for a new place, there would still be the memories he had carried from their old home in his head and which couldn't be got rid of, unlike a chair with broken legs.

When he returned to his bed he lay wondering if perhaps he shouldn't get out and about more, seeking the company of a mature woman with whom he could share the house and the rest of his life. He could take up Scottish country dancing. Vivien had been an accomplished dancer, attending the Summer School at St Andrews every year, but she hadn't been able to persuade him to attend a class with her, though she told him how dancing strathspeys and reels seemed to raise one to a new plane of pleasure – 'better than sex,' she had said with a smile. Or he could do something less strenuous, going across to Dundee for ballroom dancing lessons. A relationship with another woman of his own generation wasn't likely to have the enduring intensity of his marriage, but it would be better than the despairing feelings of loneliness he was beginning to experience every night in that house where he had been so happy and in which he had never suffered from sleeplessness until his bereavement. He used to sleep so peacefully beside his late wife that she would have to waken him in case he was late for an early lecture. But now he found himself wakening with a start in the small hours and wondering in terror where he was until he found the light switch, as if he were in a strange house.

He was only sleeping for a few hours, and there was no benefit in remaining in bed beyond six. The day that stretched in front of him was long, and by the time he had showered and shaved and made some breakfast, it was only seven, too early to go into his office to work on his book. He should have gone for an invigorating walk along the West Sands, but he seemed to be suffering from a lack of energy, both emotional and physical. He needed the company of someone young and optimistic like Rebecca, but on a platonic basis, the daughter he and Vivien had been denied.

Since there were no classes on a Wednesday afternoon, Mackilligin took Rebecca on several visits to Edinburgh, to view the collection of two hundred plaster casts, including antique ones, donated to and acquired by the College of Art in the early nineteenth century as a valuable teaching resource. Afterwards they would walk in Princes Street Gardens until it was time to go to supper in a restaurant. He felt relaxed about meeting either of her parents because this was a bona fide art excursion, a continuation of their daughter's education. He looked forward to these afternoons with Rebecca, and as they dined he saw in her face by candlelight the same innocence he had observed on the features of Hellenistic statues. On the way to the train he wanted to take her arm, but felt it would send a wrong signal.

Chapter 4

Mackilligin considered inviting Rebecca out to a restaurant in St Andrews, but in the end he decided to make her a supper. Vivien had always done the cooking, because she liked preparing dishes, and because he spent so much time at his office, working on his Hellenistic statuary book and preparing lectures. He pored over the small library of cookery books she had left, and decided that most of the recipes were beyond him. However, there was a seemingly simple recipe for venison steaks, with the assurance that one had only to set the oven to the correct temperature, then to test the meat for tenderness periodically.

When Rebecca appeared in his lecture on Friday morning he asked her to supper the following evening, and she accepted with pleasure. At nine a.m. on the Saturday, with the cobbles of Market Street washed by an overnight shower, the art historian went out with his wife's green hemp bag to do the shopping. In the smart shop with its immaculate tiled floor he took the advice of the assistant in the striped apron and brimmed white hat. Meat from deer raised on a farm without chemicals fed to boost their yield was best, he told the customer, balancing the bloody polythene packet of choice cuts on his palm.

'Serve it with cranberry sauce,' the assistant instructed him, lifting down a jar from the shelf.

Mackilligin put his purchases into the hemp bag and moved along to the next shop on his list. He had thought about strawberries for the sweet, but the season for them was finished. He met one of his colleagues and they had a short banal conversation, not about painting, but about the weather, with the Rubens expert warning that 'rain was moving across the Atlantic.'

Mackilligin went into the delicatessen, aromatic with spices, the shelves stocked with Bath Oliver biscuits and other choices of the affluent. He had an awkward conversation with the well-spoken girl (a student doing a Saturday job?) on what he should buy as a sweet for a young tooth. She sent him round the corner to a café whose ice cream attracted long queues on the summer pavements. He bought a selection of sorbets in a tub and was advised to get them into the freezer soon. He arranged to pick up the tub after he completed his shopping.

In the supermarket he pressed a melon to test its ripeness as the cookery book had advised, and decided, when the pale skin yielded to his thumbs, to serve it with the sorbet. The hemp bag over his arm, he put a small polythene sack of new potatoes into the blue plastic basket, adding to it a selection of organic vegetables. He seemed to scrutinise the shelves in the supermarket with the same intensity of concentration as he studied statues, until he found the coffee shelf in the maze of aisles and decided on a Fairtrade blend.

When the sorbet was safely in the freezer he spread out his purchases on the worktop, as if preparing to paint a still life. The book he propped on his wife's stand, like the Bible he had read from in Chapel, instructed him to tenderise the venison. He rummaged in the neat drawer for the necessary tool, but didn't know what he was looking for, so he consulted the page again and was told: 'if you don't have a tenderiser, use the prongs of a fork.'

He slid the bloody fillets from their pouch and subjected them to twenty stabbings each on the board which he had seen his wife use to dice vegetables. He laid them in the smoke-coloured casserole, shook some drops from the tall aesthetic flask of virgin olive oil that Vivien had sworn by in her culinary efforts, and set the prepared meal aside. Another page of the book warned him to leave the preparation of the vegetables to closer to the time of the meal, so as to preserve their freshness.

Vivien and he usually had a modest glass of wine with their supper. He had always bought quality, and there were half a dozen bottles of white and red she hadn't lived to enjoy in the wooden rack. He extracted the cork from a bottle of reasonably old Beaune to let it breathe before consumption.

These preparations had taken him the best part of an hour, and then he turned his attention to the dining area at the other end of the kitchen. The cottage had had a separate dining-room when they purchased it, but Vivien didn't want to carry hot casseroles across the passageway. Besides, she wanted to be able to stand at her hob and talk to her guests as she served them, so the dining space had been incorporated into the kitchen.

It was years since he had set a table, and he had to search cupboards before he found the neatly stacked linen. As he lifted down the brightly coloured cloths he recalled happy dinner parties with his wife and their friends. But he knew that on this special occasion he couldn't afford to become depressed. He chose white and blue napery, from a set given to them as a wedding present.

He decided that silver napkin rings were too old fashioned. By this time it was one thirty, and he toasted himself a slice of bread and cheese. There were still six hours before his guest stepped through the door. Should he go for a rest or for a walk along the West Sands? He would conserve his strength and go up to his bed.

Mackilligin dreamed that he was on Iona for the summer with Vivien. They were at the bay on the western side of the ocean where he had often swum with his late wife. She had stepped out of her summer dress and was running naked towards the sea while he sat on the sand, reading. He watched her swimming backwards and forwards in his line of vision as he sat working on his book on Hellenistic sculpture. As she rose from the sea, her skin sparkling in the sun, twisting the ocean from her long hair, he saw Titian's Venus Anadyomene incarnate. But as she was running towards him across the hot sand he woke up.

He was disappointed as he lay in his bed, wanting to remain in the dream because he had been so happy and fulfilled and because he knew that it would have ended in consummation. He was singing as he lathered his body in the shower cubicle, the hissing jets invigorating his skin. He felt at least ten years younger as he slid open the white doors of the wardrobe to choose what to wear that evening. Formality might intimidate his young guest, and he wanted to feel relaxed himself, so he lifted out dark blue cotton trousers and a blue checked shirt with short sleeves.

He went down to prepare the vegetables, scrubbing the carrots under the swan-necked tap and dicing them carefully on the board so as not to draw blood. The timer on the oven was beyond him, so he checked the venison page again in the cook book, which instructed him to give the tenderised meat an hour.

The meal was cooking as he made the two wine glasses shine with a cloth, and straightened a fork on the pine table. He shut the slatted blind so that passers-by wouldn't see he was entertaining a student.

Rebecca rang the bell at precisely seven thirty, by which time he had had a substantial glass of the Beaune to give him courage. He kissed her on the cheek, then took her red gown, hanging it in the hall beside his late wife's coat before leading her into the lounge, where he had ignited the imitation log gas fire because it was chilly.

'How did you spend the day?' he asked as he sat opposite her in an arm-chair.

'I was studying,' she told him, sitting with erect spine on the edge of the sofa, her hands folded on her lap, as if it were a formal interview. 'I've an essay on the Gospel of Matthew to write.'

He decided to keep clear of that subject. On their excursion to Edinburgh they had discussed religious art, but that theme was exhausted for the time being, and he was having difficulty finding a new one, so he excused himself to check the progress of the supper, hoping that the trip through to the kitchen would give him inspiration. After the meat yielded to the long-pronged fork he went back through and offered his guest a pre-prandial sherry.

'That would be very nice.'

'Sweet or dry?'

'Whatever you have, thank you.'

He brought through two glasses filled close to the brim.

'*Slainte*!' he said, holding up his glass.

'I haven't heard that toast before,' she told him, intrigued.

'It's Gaelic.'

It was time to go next door, to attend to the venison, which was perfectly cooked. He called her through as he served the meal so that they could continue talking, as his wife had done with their guests.

'This is delicious,' she complimented him.

'It's my first attempt at cooking a meal,' he confessed proudly, then, realising that it must sound chauvinistic, he added hastily: 'my wife didn't trust me in the kitchen.'

There was a look of uncertainty on her face as he moved the wine bottle towards her glass, but she allowed it to be poured.

'How is your book coming on?' she enquired.

'I've done hardly anything on it for months. I really need to get on with it. There's a certain urgency because there's a scholar at the Slade who's also writing a book on Hellenistic sculpture.'

The sorbet with the melon was a success after the tender venison, and though she put a cautionary hand over her glass, he lifted it aside, pouring more wine. He could see the transformation in her face. She was more relaxed, her shoulders down, and she talked animatedly about how much she loved St Andrews, and how grateful she was to him for taking an interest in her.

'I'm the one who should be grateful,' he told her. 'I'm honoured to have the company of a young person, who's both beautiful and talented. You remind me so much of my late wife.'

She nodded and smiled as he talked about art, but he realised that she wasn't taking in what he was saying. There was a doubt now in his mind: had he given her too much to drink? It was obvious that this was her first time tipsy. At the beginning of the evening she had been sitting on the sofa with her legs together, but now they were apart, and she had kicked off the practical flat-heeled shoes.

'So what's the programme for tomorrow?' he enquired.

'Chapel, the choir.'

'But you like that.'

'Yes I like it, but it's a big commitment in the week.' She hesitated. 'Sometimes I wish –'

'You wish?' he gave her time.

'I wish that I hadn't joined the choir. But my father was in it when he was here.'

'Listen: you don't have to do everything that your father tells you,' he urged her. 'You're a woman now, in charge of your own life.' As he was speaking he moved towards her and sat down beside her on the sofa. Later, when he came to reconstruct this critical moment – and he would do so many times – the factor he was searching for would always be elusive. But somehow his delight in her company had turned into desire. However it happened, he was on the sofa beside her, his arm round her shoulders. What was intended as a reassuring hug became an embrace as he drew her towards him.

He kissed her on the mouth.

His guest was taken aback. Her limit was a modest mulled wine at Christmas time, but she had consumed a sherry and two substantial glasses of wine. Her head was light, her vision affected. The suddenness of the kiss shocked her, but it also gave her a feeling she had never had before, it being her first kiss on the mouth from a male.

The art historian ran his hand up his student's thigh and felt it yielding. His fingers groped the no-frills cotton knickers, and she had the first climax of her life, there on the sofa, within seconds. It was too crude, too uncomfortable to use the sofa, so he took her hand upstairs to the bedroom he had shared with his late wife. He lifted the drab kimono over her head and was pulling down the cotton knickers and tights.

'No,' she told him, gripping these garments.

'Why not?'

'Because it isn't right.'

She had been raised a devout Catholic, and had been warned in the home and at church that pre-marital sex was a sin. Her seducer knew from her stiffening body that this was a decisive moment, but to stop now was to thwart his urgent desire. He held her by the shoulders, kissing her on the mouth. He hadn't bought contraceptives, but he didn't withdraw. It was over in thirty seconds, and when he should have been utterly relaxed, lying beside her, the consequences of what he had done were making him rigid with terror. *She could accuse me of filling her up with drink and then raping her*. He saw the headlines of the scandal: dismissed from his post, sent to prison, his book on Hellenistic sculpture abandoned.

He turned his head on the pillow to look at her, and saw a tear on the side of her face.

'I'm sorry,' he whispered.

She turned her head and smiled, catching his hand and squeezing it.

'God, I love you,' he told her, and was inside her again, this time guided by her, but withdrawing before the critical moment.

They lay together, shoulder to shoulder.

'You're very pensive,' he remarked.

'I'm thinking about my upbringing.'

'You have a very pleasant home and friendly parents.'

She turned her face on the pillow towards him, speaking with a passion he hadn't heard before, as if the rupture of her hymen had released more than blood. She had found her confessor at last.

'I've never been allowed to make any decisions for myself. My mother dictated when I was to be taken to the baths, and who I was to swim with. My clothes were bought for me without my preferences being taken into consideration. Away from school my friends were allowed to wear denims and trainers, but my mother considered these to be sloppy.

Some of my friends had pierced ears and nose-studs – "disfigurements," she called them.'

He wondered if he should interrupt this tirade, but he was intrigued, and she was even more attractive in her anger, a side he hadn't seen before.

'I started piano lessons when I was four. I loved it, but when I was nine I was told that I was going to study the organ instead, because my father played it in the chapel we went to. He gave me extra tuition in classics, because that's what he wanted me to study at St Andrews, his alma mater. Then my mother decided that I was to study theology. When I asked her what I would do with such a degree, she said: "you can teach in a Catholic school." You have no idea what it is to live in that house, which looks so peaceful and welcoming. My mother makes wholesome dishes, with plenty of vegetables, and won't allow me an electric blanket because she read that it emits radiation, even when it's switched off. I live in a house where there has to be absolute silence whenever there's sport on television.'

'But you're away from it now, at university,' he pointed out. 'You can eat and wear what you like.'

'Oh no: my mother chose my clothes for St Andrews. My father said it was a cold place by the North Sea, so there had to be sweaters in the case she packed for me, as well as some of my father's classics texts from his university course. I wanted to come by train, but I was driven here, and my room in McIntosh Hall was inspected. It was my mother who hung my clothes on the rail and folded them into the allotted drawers. She even inspected the showers.'

It was not often that the art historian was lost for words. He had had to deal with temperamental students down the years, but this was different: this was a young woman in another subject pouring out her heart – and her anger – to him as she lay beside him in his bed. He was pleased in a perverse way, because it showed that she trusted him.

'But you've settled into McIntosh,' he pointed out.

'Not really. I've found it difficult making friends in the Hall, because we dress differently and have different interests. I felt such a fool, not knowing who the Arctic Monkeys are. I wear these skirts that my mother chose for me, while the other students in the hall are wearing denims with ragged bottoms and patches on the knees. They have mobile phones, but I'm not allowed one, not only because of the expense but also because my mother's worried about radiation damage to the brain.'

'What you need to do on Monday is to go out and buy yourself a pair of denims,' he told her.

She looked at him in astonishment. 'I wouldn't know where to go.'

'One of the students in the Hall will take you.'

'And suppose I'm wearing them when my mother comes on an inspection visit?'

'Tell her you have a new dress code – a modern one. Stay here for the night,' he urged her.

She took his hand and laid it on her breast.

'I'd better not. They might miss me in the Hall and think I've been murdered. Thank you for a wonderful evening, Alan.'

Her use of his name thrilled him, like a caress. He lay watching the kimono slipping down her substantial breasts and broad appealing hips. He dressed and went downstairs with her.

'I'll drive you back to Hall.'

'No, I'd rather walk to get fresh air.'

He held her tightly before he opened the door, and when she had gone he stood with his forehead against the wood before turning the key. When he went through to load the supper things into the dishwasher the terror of what he had done returned, and he sat on the sofa with a stiff whisky. By seducing one of his students he had not only betrayed the Platonic ideals of respect for women and their bodies which he had discovered from his classical studies and which he had practised in his marriage: he had also betrayed his late wife in their home, which had always been a place of harmony and honesty. In his remorse and terror he could see Rebecca stumbling into McIntosh Hall, wailing to the warden that she had been raped by Professor Mackilligin, having been enticed to his house and plied with drink, which she wasn't used to. His imagination, heightened by the whisky and the sex, was so vivid that he could see the warden picking up the phone to summon the police. They could be round at his door within ten minutes, he told himself as he gulped whisky, its fire hitting his throat making him cough.

Rebecca stopped on the cobbles outside St Salvator's Chapel to inhale the night air as she looked up at the stars beyond the steeple. She was elated, the heat of her seduction still in her body. She had found a lover as well as a mentor. When she reached her room she took off her clothes and stretched out on the bed. She had never dreamt that sex would be like this. Her mother had given her so many lectures about how predatory men were, only interested in getting into the one place. But what her mother hadn't told her was that there was tenderness too in the act. She swung down her legs and went to a drawer. Taking out scissors, she grasped her long hair and began to hack it off.

Chapter 5

Mackilligin waited up until one a.m., when the dishwasher had completed its cycle and the whisky bottle was empty. He stumbled up the stairs, hitting his shoulder on the frame of the door of his wife's studio, grasping the handle and pushing. The pieces from the stained glass were lying on the floor, like a coloured fragmented pool in the light coming in from the landing. He went down on his knees to try to pick them up, but there was no coordination between his eye and hand because of the amount of alcohol he had consumed. It was as if the shapes were stuck to the floor.

He propped himself against the lintel as he began a drunken dialogue with the strewn glass.

'I've been so lonely, missing you so much, I couldn't go on. I know, I know – I shouldn't have done it in our house, and with a woman so young. But you've got to understand, Vivien, that what happened tonight has saved my sanity. I honestly think I was in danger of doing something to myself, because my life lost its direction and purpose after you died. Oh yes, I know, I know (he held up his palms) I should have immersed myself in my book. This young woman will help me to get back on track; you'll see. If I hadn't drunk so much tonight I would have opened up the laptop and resumed the sculpture book where I left off before you became really sick. Yes, yes, she's too young for me: I could be her grandfather.' He spread his hands. 'But we're attracted to each other, so what does the difference in age matter? Yes, I took advantage of her; she's had no experience of sex. I supplied the booze but it was her choice, how much to drink, her choice to go to bed with me. Baby snatching? I don't think that's fair, Vivien. OK, OK. But she's a fully developed woman, capable of bearing children. I know, I know, we couldn't have any because of your blocked tubes, but that was before the days of implanting eggs, so we had to find compensation in other things – your stained glass, my fascination with Hellenistic sculpture. Do I miss not having children? Of course I do, but I never said it to you because I knew how much it would hurt you. Oh hell.'

He shut the door on his last vestiges of guilt and climbed the half dozen stairs to the bedroom. The duvet was thrown back and he noticed the bloody evidence of Rebecca's initiation. Rather than change the linen, he decided to sleep in it as a sign of his new love, and his repose was deep and without dreams, not even disturbed by the clamour of gulls tearing apart a black rubbish sack further up the street, spilling the expensive offal on the cobbles.

He rose at seven and had a prolonged shower to try to wash the alcohol out of his system, remembering to put the soiled sheet in the washing machine so that Marjorie wouldn't notice it when she changed his bed. He couldn't look at a cooked breakfast, but he squeezed an orange and took two aspirins. That was when he had the idea that he should rejoin the staff procession in St Salvator's Chapel after such a long absence. He knew that he wasn't doing it for reasons of atonement after the seduction, but because he wanted to see Rebecca again. He went round to his office and lifted his gown and academic hood from the cupboard, joining the procession lined up in the cloisters in their robes and tasselled caps and following the historic mace into a stall in the ornate pews.

To his left, beyond the chaplain in his blue cassock, was the mouldering tomb of Bishop Kennedy, founder of the College. Opposite him, under the large stained glass windows, were the students who had been able to turn out of their beds after parties that had gone on into the small hours. He scanned the faces of the earnest, the anxious, and the unconcerned. University was about having a good time as well as obtaining a degree, the suspension of responsibilities. He hadn't been the same in his Edinburgh days, he recalled as the choir above rose to sing Tallis.

He looked up, but couldn't see Rebecca standing under the gilded organ pipes. His terror had returned. She must have been traumatised by his seduction of her, and the warden would have called the doctor. The police would be waiting for him outside the Chapel, he convinced himself as he rose from his pew for the exit of the academic procession following the big Bible, his legs weakening with each step. But there was no policeman, and he was hurrying away when he was detained by an emeritus professor who asked him how he was and who proceeded to recall the loss of his own wife twenty years before. Desperate to get away and not listening to a word, Mackilligin saw the choir emerging from the Chapel. A young woman smiled at him, and he saw that it was Rebecca, but with her hair shorn.

Mackilligin could have gone down on his knees on the flagstones and said a prayer of gratitude. The tradition was that sherry was served in the Hebdomadar's Room, so he went up the stairs with the other academics and the choir.

'What's brought you back after so many years, Alan?' an Old Testament scholar asked.

'I began to worry.'

'About what?'

'My soul.'

'I'm sure your soul is in good shape.'

'Not as good as yours.'

'I don't know. Being a Biblical scholar isn't a sign of exceptional piety. How are you bearing up in your bereavement?'

'It's difficult, adjusting to being on one's own,' he confessed.

'You must come round to us for supper soon. I'll send you an e-mail after I've consulted my wife about a date.'

When the choir came up the stairs he smiled at Rebecca, but decided that it was prudent not to talk with her. He saw how radiant she looked, and he knew that everything was going to be all right. On the way out, as he passed her, he whispered: 'tonight?' and she nodded.

When Rebecca knocked his door at seven she was wearing denims.

'Where did you get these?' he asked in surprise as she spun round for his approval.

'I took the bus to Dundee this afternoon and bought some new clothes.'

'They suit you,' he complimented her, feeling a surge of desire, the way they clung to her inviting hips. He offered to cook supper for her but she had already eaten in Hall.

'I like your hair,' he told her as he touched it.

'My mother always insisted on me keeping it long, even though all my friends at school had theirs shortened.'

'So having your hair cut and buying denims are acts of rebellion,' he smiled.

'You could call it that.'

'And will it extend to other things?'

'All my life I've been told what to do – or rather, what not to do. It's time for a change. I'm going to wear what I like, go where I like and when I like. So I'm not going home next weekend.'

'Have you told them?' he asked, intrigued, handing her a sherry.

'Not yet. But I will, in the course of the week. I always phone, but this time I'm going to e-mail my father at school. My mother refuses to get into computers. The phone's her thing. She's never off it, to her friends, arranging to meet them for coffee and the roster for the charity shop she works in two afternoons a week.'

He sat beside her and clinked glasses with her.

'To your liberation.'

When he took her upstairs he had to exert himself to pull down the tight pristine denims, and after their frenetic coupling he lay beside her. His remorse at seducing a woman a third of his age had been replaced by the same feeling of peace he had known after Vivien and he had made love on Iona, lying together, listening to the clean ocean washing up on the sand, waking in the twilight to go through with bare feet to the kitchen where she prepared supper from the pail of seafood left at the door by an islander. The truth was that Rebecca was making him feel young and vigorous, as though he were starting out again, with his academic career in front of him. That evening in the house in St Andrews he felt that life still held promise and fulfilment, though he was a widower. He wanted to get back to his book on Hellenistic sculpture, to use the contentment and tranquillity he was drawing from his relationship with his young lover to gain new insight into that art form.

'Are you happy?' she asked, holding his hand.

'I'm very happy. And you?'

'Very happy.' She snuggled up against his shoulder.

The sex was wonderful, with her considerate lover concerned with her pleasure as much as his own. And his conversation stimulated hers in a way that her male contemporaries could not, because they lacked the knowledge and insight that came with maturity. But would she disclose her sin of fornication the next time she went to confession? Perhaps there wouldn't be a next time, because she blamed the strictness of her religious upbringing for her unhappiness, as well as her domineering parents.

Next day the rejuvenated art historian purchased trainers in a sports shop – footwear he wouldn't have been seen in previously – and the following morning he left the house at seven and went jogging on the West Sands in the company of early risers from the halls of residence. He had to get fit because he was expending a lot of energy in bed with a young woman who was strenuous in her demands. He ran for a mile towards the estuary of the Eden, the breeze at his back, the stains of his exertions in his armpits. As his trainers pounded the compacted sand he was thinking how lucky he was to get this new lease of life, to be lifted out of the depressing inertia of bereavement. But he also knew that he had to be prudent. Many staff took students for coffee, to discuss coursework or personal problems with them, but he couldn't do that too often without provoking damaging gossip. However, there was satisfaction in their secret meetings in his house, as if he were defeating the mores of the university town which, he was only now beginning to realise, could be stultifying. But he knew that he had to be careful that his neighbours didn't talk about the visits of a young woman to his house.

He also found that his lover was inspiring him to resume his book. When he had free time he sat writing in his office, and on the evenings when Rebecca wasn't in his bed he wrote on his laptop at the kitchen table, a glass of nutritious juice within reach. When he went round the supermarket, it was with a trolley, not a basket, because he was now shopping for two. Though she reminded him that she could eat in Hall, he insisted on cooking for both of them, and was becoming interested in the preparation and presentation of food. He carried his hemp bags of shopping through the wynds to his kitchen, where there was a new healthier cook-book on the stand. He was also sleeping well, without the assistance of whisky. He hadn't felt so happy and confident since the early years of his marriage, when life seemed so full of promise, before the financial cutbacks and relentless research scrutiny took part of the pleasure and fulfilment out of an academic career. Five star rating was a necessity to attract overseas students, and they brought big fees. He heard more and more American and Asian accents in the streets of St Andrews.

In his time as a student final examinations had been spread over several days and involved a substantial number of hours. Now with continuous assessment and a wide choice of modules they could be over in a few hours. Mackilligin doubted if students knew as much nowadays, but it certainly wasn't a question to raise at Senate.

He had heard stories of St Andrews in the 1930s from Ronald Cant, the university's chronicler who had come as a young historian. The student population had been under a thousand, and staff played rounds of golf with their students before coming off the links at five o' clock for a civilised sherry.

'We had a lot of well-heeled students of both sexes,' Cant recalled, standing in a wynd whose historic buildings he had helped to save, the collar of his frayed tweed coat turned up against the snell wind from the sea, a tweed cap shielding the large curve of his bald head. 'In some cases there wasn't a necessity to take a degree. They came to St Andrews for a gloss of learning and to be turned into gentlemen and eligible young ladies. Now there are five thousand students and good degrees are a necessity.'

Despite the increased teaching load and the research targets, Mackilligin was happy at St Andrews, and now, the happiest he had been since his arrival because of the young lover in his life. He had settled in his mind the guilt about a liaison so short a time after his wife's death. Vivien would approve because the last thing she would have wanted for him was to be left lonely and bereft.

One evening Rebecca was sitting at his kitchen table, making calculations on a pad.

'What are you doing?' he asked, intrigued.

'Working out my finances.'

'Are they that bad?' he jested. 'Your parents don't look short.'

'They told me that they would meet all my expenses at university, out of money my mother was left by her father. He was a Writer to the Signet in Edinburgh, with an office in the New Town which Sir Walter Scott frequented – or so my mother claims. Her name was Arthurson, my father's a Campbell, so that's why they became Campbell-Arthurson when they married. They told me that they didn't want me taking out student loans and leaving university with debts.'

'That's very generous of them,' he said sincerely. 'There are a lot of students here with big debts and poor prospects of a job when they graduate. I don't know how they're going to be able to buy a house or start a family with that millstone round their necks. You're one of the few fortunate ones.'

'Ah, but my parents' largesse comes with a condition: I have to keep an account of my expenditure, and my mother checks it. I don't even have a bank account because all the bills - for the Hall, my living expenses - are paid for by her. I'm allowed so much for books, but if there are extras I have to ask for more money. I have to take this notebook home with me to be checked.'

'I don't believe you,' he said incredulously.

'Have a look.' She held out the notebook. 'These ticks are my mother's, not mine. I'm told that it's not meanness on their part, but to teach me the value of money. I asked for more money because I'd bought the denims and some tops, but she refused me, so I e-mailed my father. I was called to the phone in the Hall last night by my mother. "What's the meaning of this?" The meaning of what, mother? "Going behind my back to ask your father for money when I refused you. What do you need more money for?" Text books, I lied. "But we bought all your text books for you at the beginning of term. Besides, you always phone. Why are you suddenly e-mailing?" Because I have an essay to write and since I was in the university library, near a computer, I thought I'd e-mail. "So you can't come home this weekend to see your parents?" I told you, mother, I've an essay to write. There's a lot of work, and I don't want to fall behind. "Your father will help you with the essay." I know he would, but I'm supposed to write it myself. He won't be sitting beside me when I have to do exams. "But you'll be home the following weekend?" That depends on my work-load. I'll come home as soon as I can. Then I had a brainwave, Alan. I told her: I joined the choir at the beginning of the term because daddy was in it when he was at St Andrews and because he likes singing. If I'm in Edinburgh I miss the choir and the practice before the service. Do you want me to give up the choir and come home? And there's another consideration: I can't study on a crowded train when I'm travelling backwards and forwards to Edinburgh, and you do want me to get a First, like daddy did? That did the trick, Alan, because she said: "The proudest moment of our lives will be to watch our daughter walking down the aisle in the Younger Hall to receive her first class honours in classics and theology. And are you getting plenty of greens?"'

Rebecca giggled and threw the notebook on the table. 'It would be funny if it weren't so pathetic. Evidently I've to be sent vitamin supplements. And then she said: "Are you remembering, when you're doing your washing in the machine, to separate the whites from the colours, otherwise the whites will go grey?" I'm doing that, I told her. "Don't set the iron too high or you'll scorch your clothes." I'm careful, I said. What I would have liked to have told her was: listen, I'm a woman now, at a university where I'd imagine many students are having sex. Just lay off, will you, and let me live my own life?'

'But you didn't.'

'No I didn't, because I don't have the courage – yet. But I'm getting it from you.'

'From me?' he queried, surprised.

'Yes, you're giving me strength and confidence.'

They went up to bed, and she didn't return to the Hall until close to midnight. As he stepped out into the narrow street with her he pointed to the lighted window of a neighbour's house and put a finger to his lips. She appeared next evening, to tell him what had happened. She had slept so soundly that she had missed breakfast, and when her door was rapped at eleven she shouted to the caller to go away, then heard the indignant reply: 'I will not go away!' It was her mother. When she saw her daughter's short hair she was furious, reminding her that she had tended it so carefully since Rebecca was a child. Rebecca told her that most of the students had short hair.

'And you wanted to be like them. The hairdresser was always saying what beautiful hair you had and yet you cut it off just because other sloppy women – some of whom I saw just now downstairs, slouching about, looking like tarts – wear their hair shorn. You'll not let a pair of scissors near it until it grows again, which will take months.'

While she was speaking her daughter had pulled on her denims. Her mother told her to take them off, but she refused.

'Because everyone else goes about in them, looking like tramps, is that it? Is this your way of repaying us after sending you to an expensive school to teach you manners and build your character? If your father saw you just now he would go mad.'

'But he isn't here, mother. He'll be running round a rugby pitch somewhere with a whistle in his mouth.'

'What in God's name has got into you, girl?'

'You're living in a past father's told you about, mother. When he was here at St Andrews there were still students wearing hems below their knees and mortar boards, and the men were in corduroys and tweed jackets and smoked pipes. It changed long ago. There's been a revolution and you both don't know anything about it. Young people don't live and dress any more the way you want me to live and dress.'

'Are you seeing someone?' she asked her daughter.

'What did you answer?' Mackilligin wanted to know.

'I told her that I wasn't seeing anyone, and even if I were, what would the harm be in that, so long as it doesn't interfere with my studies?' "Because young women can be taken advantage of," she said.'

'Am I taking advantage of you?' Mackilligin asked as lightly as he could.

'Of course not; you're a good influence on me. I suppose they're being over-protective. I was taken by the hand to the junior school every morning and fetched in the afternoon. When I was at senior school I was dropped off by my father on his way to his work, and picked up in the late afternoon. If I had a violin lesson, or was playing lacrosse, he sat in his car, correcting exercises with his red pen, waiting patiently for me. I was escorted to dentists, doctors, libraries, and had to swim close to him in the private baths. He dreams of me becoming headmistress of a noted girls' private school, with the title of doctor for a prize-winning thesis on a classical text.'

'And what does your mother dream of?' Mackilligin asked.

'She's always wanted me to be a nun.'

'I don't believe you.'

'I'm serious, Alan. She's incredibly religious. We used to go every second summer to Rome. She can't pass a church without going into it.'

'But surely she wants grandchildren,' he asked, puzzled.

'I've a suspicion that my mother was planning to be a nun when she met my father and was swept off her feet. That's why she wants to fulfil her thwarted ambition through me.'

'Do *you* want to be a nun?' he asked.

'I did, when I was younger. I loved my Confirmation dress, with the veil, and I love the scent of incense. But I don't have that ambition now. I want to live in the real world, to experience the sorrows as well as the joys. But you see now why she keeps me on such a tight rein.'

She's too late now, her lover thought, but didn't articulate his sentiments. What she had told him about her mother's aspirations for her placed an even bigger responsibility on his shoulders for having seduced her. He could see how she had taken strength and confidence from their relationship to challenge her domineering parents. But had he damaged her future?

Chapter 6

When Rebecca wasn't in the front row of his lecture Mackilligin didn't feel inspired, and when he was at home alone he felt depressed and seemed to lack energy, as though he were drawing his energy from her. Their love-making (he hated the clinical term sex, which conveyed nothing of the tenderness involved) was getting better and better.

'Stroke my back,' she would request, and he would lie behind her, tracing his fingers on her unblemished skin.

She was lying naked on her side on the bed, and Mackilligin beside her could see her reflection in the mirror on the dressing-table, an image which reminded him powerfully of Velasquez's painting *The Toilet of Venus*, with the reclining nude regarding her face in the mirror held up for her by Cupid.

'How are your theological studies?'

'Going very well. I'm getting good grades for the essays.'

'How is Hall?'

'I'm much happier because I'm making new friends.'

'Not male, I hope?'

'A few men. Mostly females. I go to their rooms.'

'What kind of things do you discuss?'

'I don't tell them that my lover is a professor in Art History and an expert on Hellenistic sculpture, that's for sure,' she replied with a laugh that moved her shoulders under his hand. 'We talk about various things – how we're enjoying St Andrews, and the state of the world. Most of them have part-time jobs, and I'm going to get one too.'

'Why?' he asked, sitting up.

'Because I want some extra money. As I told you, my parents keep me on a very tight budget.'

'Have you looked for a job?' he asked apprehensively.

'One of my friends in the Hall has found me one, in a coffee shop. I'm going to be working there two evenings a week and at weekends.'

'That means you won't be able to come here,' he said in alarm.

'Yes I will. I'll come an evening in the week and on Saturday, except that I may be a bit late, because I'll probably have to work until the place closes.' She turned to face him. 'Alan, I need to stand up to my parents and become more independent. I told you, they've controlled almost every aspect of my life since I was a child.'

'Will you tell them you're working part-time in a coffee shop?' her lover asked.

'Oh no, because they'd be horrified, a clever daughter studying theology selling coffees. My mother would come up to St Andrews, walk into the coffee shop and haul me out.'

Her decision to take a part-time job depressed him, and after she had zipped up her denims and departed he sat downstairs with a whisky, considering the implications. If she were standing behind the counter of a coffee shop she was bound to meet someone attractive of her own age. Would she tell him, if she went out with a student? Probably, because she was an honest person, the way she spoke about the negative influence of her parents on her life. How could he prevent her taking a job? By creating one for her? Now that was an idea. He could pay her as a research assistant for his book, pretending that the money came from a grant. But she would wonder why he hadn't proposed this arrangement before, and would work out that he was anxious about her meeting someone of her own generation in the coffee house, which was always filled with students when he passed it.

As he poured himself another whisky he knew that he was going to encounter such problems in his relationship with Rebecca, and that he would probably lose her. The age difference was too great, a figure which he couldn't bring to mind without depressing himself even more. He had to find a way of keeping her away from men of her own generation. But that was absurd, because there were several thousand male students at the university, and she was bound to get to know some of them, now that she was no longer sitting in McIntosh Hall, studying classics in the strict regime imposed by her parents. He had liberated her by seducing her and giving her confidence, thereby ironically making himself vulnerable to her defection with a younger man. Such fears would rise to torture him when he was alone at home, or preparing a lecture in his office, but he knew that it was the price he had to pay for falling in love with a woman a third of his age.

He also knew that he couldn't risk being seen in public in St Andrews with his student lover. Nor could he go on the train with her to Edinburgh too often in case colleagues were travelling to do research. But on a Wednesday afternoon when neither of them had classes he drove her up into Perthshire. They walked hand in hand through the autumnal woods, using a tree to make love against.

'When do you start work in the coffee shop?' he wanted to know, because the thought of it had been plaguing him.

'At the weekend. I'm going to work from ten o' clock till six on Saturday, then come to see you.'

'What happens if your mother turns up unexpectedly, as she did last time?'

'She won't know where to find me. She'll think that I'm working in the library.'

He saw that his obsession with her job in the coffee shop was in danger of affecting their relationship. He couldn't risk losing her by appearing as a jealous elderly man. He took her to supper in a small hotel in a village, where they had the table by the open fire, the blazing logs raised in an ironwork basket. They ate fresh fish and drank mineral water as they talked. That was another attraction of their relationship – the diversity of topics he brought up, as if he were educating her in subjects she wasn't studying.

'What do you think about climate change?' he asked her.

'I've read about it but haven't given it much thought.'

'You should,' he urged. 'It's going to affect your life.'

'In what way?'

'In many ways. The polar caps are melting and will raise sea levels. Low-lying areas like Bangladesh are likely to be swamped, millions made homeless.'

'How will that affect us here?' she asked as she ate.

'Well, these Third World countries will have to have massive financial assistance. They'll have to be compensated for being denied the opportunities to develop into advanced industrial states, as we have done and which has caused so much damage to the environment. And scientists are predicting a huge migration of wildlife. In twenty years time people could be slapping mosquitoes off their skins in St Andrews. It's my generation that has done this, Rebecca,' he added passionately. 'We've been profligate, putting carbon dioxide into the atmosphere through driving and flying.'

'So what's to be done?'

'There are two schools of thought among scientists. One school says that the damage is already done and that it's irreversible. The other school maintains that we can still limit the damage by restricting our driving and all sorts of other things.'

'Which means that we shouldn't have come up here today.'

'You're perfectly right. That's how difficult it's going to be.'

He saw that she hadn't thought about these matters. She was young and she wanted as much out of life as possible. Worrying about the future of the planet was for older people like himself – those who had abused it. It was like consciousness of ageing. When you were young you couldn't conceive of what it was going to be like to be old. To her, sitting opposite him drinking coffee, he knew that he must seem old to her, and that was why it was going to be difficult to hold onto her. If she left him now he knew that he would age drastically and wouldn't be able to form a relationship with a woman of his own age. In a way he was in thrall to her, like Thomas the Rhymer in the Scots ballad who kisses the beautiful woman he encounters and is carried off to Fairyland. But such stories usually ended in sorrow and abandonment, and he couldn't allow that to happen. He knew, however, that he had to face up to the fact that one day she would finish her degree at St Andrews. He would be three years older by them, approaching pensionable age.

As he watched the way the light was shining on her hair his hands were trembling, the coffee cup audible on the saucer. He was overcome with a feeling of terror that he would be left alone in the future; retired from teaching; the Hellenistic book unfinished; shuffling along Market Street with the green bag for his shopping. There would be long lonely nights in a house eerie with the shadows of two cherished women.

'What are you thinking about?' his lover asked.

'I'm thinking how beautiful you are, Rebecca.'

'I think I'm quite ordinary.'

'You'll never be that to me.'

On Saturday Rebecca began work in the coffee shop. It was a busy place, satisfying the demand for frothing concoctions. He was out shopping for their supper and saw her shapely figure through the window as she worked the machine, and on an impulse he joined the queue. She smiled at him when he asked for a small decaffeinated coffee and a cake, and he carried his purchases to a table where he sat pretending to read the *Scotsman*. But he was watching male students chatting to her as she took their orders, her animated face irritating him and plunging him into a foul mood. Without acknowledging her he left the place, deafening with piped music and chatter, and went home, to sit pensively on the steps up into the garden. He was going to have to overcome his jealousy. But how?

Vivien had been deep into spiritual matters and had amassed a considerable library of books on religions and belief systems from all over the world. He recalled one evening when he was ranting to Vivien against a colleague who, he perceived, had done him an injustice.

'You need to manage your anger,' his wife had warned him and had disappeared upstairs, returning with a book which she placed on the supper table in front of him.

'What's this?' he asked suspiciously.

'It's about meditation. It's what you need to do.'

Several times he had opened the door to her studio and found her sitting cross-legged on a cushion on the floor, a fragrant candle burning in front of her. She explained to him after her session that she had been meditating, in order to induce a state of calm and contemplation to help her in realising her vision in stained glass.

'I'll show you how, Alan.'

He had been reluctant, but followed her up the stairs and sat on a cushion opposite her.

'Don't close your eyes, otherwise you'll fall asleep,' she cautioned. 'Look down at an angle of about forty five degrees at the candle flame. The object is to empty the mind of mundane thoughts and worries and to achieve a state of peace.'

After fifteen minutes sitting cross-legged opposite her (painful on his thighs), he reported that he couldn't empty his mind.

'You can't expect results after one session. You've got to persist, and even if thoughts come into your head, that doesn't matter. What you mustn't do is to *consciously* think and pursue a thought.'

He had tried several sessions, sitting opposite her, beginning to feel calm and relaxed as the candle flame seemed to grow until it was burning inside his head. But he began to make excuses that he had work to do, and had stopped sitting. Now, as he sat on the step in the garden in the unseasonably mild November evening, he decided to try again. On his hands and knees he picked up all the pieces of his late wife's uncompleted window design which he had pushed off her table in his anger at her death. He took the cushion she had sat on, and went downstairs to light the remains of the last candle she had used.

He stripped down to his boxer shorts in the bedroom before going into the studio, to sit cross-legged on the cushion and regard the candle flame. Vivien had taught him to be conscious of the rhythmic sound of his breath, but as he tried to enter a state of meditation he kept seeing in his head his lover standing in her denims at the counter in the coffee shop. At the end of half an hour she was still there, now chatting to a male student. Mackilligin sat with clenched fists, frustrated that he couldn't control his emotions. He was a sixty plus man with the jealousy of a youth, and he knew that he was going to have to overcome it if the relationship was going to continue. Rebecca had to have a life of her own when she wasn't with him. She wasn't a kept woman at his beck and call.

He blew out the candle and went downstairs. When he started drinking by himself after Vivien's death he had become morbid, recalling the good times together, especially on Iona. At the beginning, when they met as students, he was invited to the house on the island to share family holidays with her parents and her sister and brother. Her father Alasdair had inherited the house from an aunt with whom he had been holidaying since boyhood. It was built of substantial blocks of whitewashed stone to withstand the gales that swept across the exposed island, a vulnerability that the marauding Norsemen had taken advantage of when they came to loot and torch the wood and wattle monastery and slaughter its inhabitants. The roof of the family house was red-painted corrugated iron which rattled under the rain driven in from the Atlantic. Two acres of croft ground went with the house, and a local farmer had sheep on it, apart from an area round the dwelling which Vivien's mother Catherine had staked off as a small garden, planting hedges in the sandy soil to protect the flowers and vegetables from the wind. Every summer she returned she found that the hedges had disappeared, whirled into the sky by a storm, but she persevered, and eventually her plantings had secure roots. Mackilligin was sent out to dig up the lettuce for the supper, which, on calm evenings, was served in the garden at a long table knocked together from planks salvaged from the ocean.

More whisky in his St Andrews home brought him back to that hospitable table on Iona. Though Alasdair his future father-in-law was a minister who lectured in theology, the conversation was never solemn after he had given thanks for the produce of land and sea which they were about to eat. The main course was clams dredged up that afternoon, their polished shells prised open, the briny tang of the contents lingering in the mouth. Alcohol was not drunk at this table, as the theologian at its head believed that the atmosphere of the island was sufficiently intoxicating. Vivien's older sister Charlotte talked about a traveller she had met on the ferry when she went across to the island of Mull for provisions in the morning. He was a black man from Africa who had come on pilgrimage to Iona, and had stood on the deck of the ferry crossing the sound, playing the pipes, a balmoral angled on his frizzled head. Vivien laughed at the image, but not in a cynical way.

While Catherine brought out the large aluminium teapot Alasdair went indoors to fetch a small melodeon which his uncle had taught him to play in that same house on days when the barefooted boy couldn't get out because of wind and rain. He thrust his hands through the straps and began to play. But it wasn't a selection of hymns at the close of day that the *al fresco* diners were getting. He played a selection of Scottish airs, and joined in, singing 'The Deil's Awa wi' the Exciseman' on the sacred isle, the bellows going in and out until the player's hands began to fade with the light.

Decades on, Mackilligin, older now than his long-deceased musical Iona host, found himself singing the same song in his St Andrews house as he swung the whisky glass in his solitary ceilidh.

Chapter 7

Rebecca took the Saturday off from the coffee house and went home. She had decided that she wasn't going to wear her denims and force a confrontation with her parents, so she put on one of the ankle-length tweed skirts that her mother had bought for her. Mackilligin waved to her from his parked car as she crossed the bridge at Leuchars Station in the windy Sunday on her return from Edinburgh. He opened the boot for the purchases imposed on her by her mother, and when they were safely inside the vehicle they embraced.

'So you didn't have a good visit?' he prompted as he drove her to St Andrews.

'It was bloody awful. I was told by my father that following the herd wasn't a sound enough reason for cutting my hair, which, my mother claimed, was my crowning glory. I told him that I'd cut it because it's easier to dry after I've had my work-out at the sports centre. That seemed to satisfy him, because he's a fitness fanatic who goes out jogging for half an hour before going to school. He's been placed in the high list in half a dozen marathons. I wanted to visit a school friend, but for the sake of peace I had to trail round the shops after my mother, who wanted to buy me more clothes, though I told her I didn't need any more. What else? We had bowls of nourishing tomato soup in the restaurant at the top of Jenners, before lugging the carrier bags to her car. My father was watching a rugby match between Fettes and the Academy in the afternoon. My mother's addicted to

EWTN, the Catholic satellite channel, and I had to sit through a documentary on female saints last night after supper. This morning I went with them to church, then home for lunch and the Sunday papers. You know, I feel I no longer belong in that house. Anyway, what have you been doing?'

'I tried to do some work on my book, but I missed you so much I was disorientated.'

'I won't go back until the Christmas holiday.'

'I was hoping you'd spend some of the time in St Andrews.'

'That would be difficult. They'd get suspicious, because they know – since they pay the bills – that the hall of residence is closed.'

'You could say that you're staying with a friend - a female friend,' he suggested.

'I'd be subjected to an interrogation. Who is this person? Is she a Catholic? Suitable company for you? And is your own home not good enough for you at Christmastime?'

'I can come down to Edinburgh to see you.'

'That would be dangerous. One of my parents' friends could see us and report back, and then all hell would break loose.'

'Then where can we meet?' he asked, exasperated.

'We can talk about that later,' she reassured him.

He had left the heater and electric blanket on in the bedroom, and within five minutes of entering the house he was inside her and being held by the urgency of her desire.

'Are you working in the coffee shop this week?' he enquired.

'On Wednesday and Friday evenings, and all day

Saturday.'

'I still wish you wouldn't and let me help you financially.'

'No, I have to do this by myself,' she told him earnestly. 'I have to become independent of them and find the strength to stand up to them and make a life for myself, where all the decisions are mine alone.'

Three nights later she was back in the coffee shop. He decided to go for a walk in the blustery evening, but knew that it wasn't for the sake of his constitution, but so that he could stop at the brightly lit window of the coffee shop, not only to admire his lover behind the counter, but to make sure that no young male customer spoke with her for longer than it took her to serve the chosen coffee. When she turned to look out of the window he hurried away. Instead of going home (which he felt would be too lonely because of his despondent mood) he went into his office and switched on the light-box to select slides for future lectures. But he couldn't concentrate. This wasn't going to work unless Rebecca moved in with him. But that would cause a scandal and force him to relinquish his professorship. He had to be sensible about this and stop behaving like an adolescent. There was the Hellenistic sculpture book to complete, lectures to be prepared.

The following morning Rebecca was in the front row for Mackilligin's lecture.

'You remember that we looked at the copy of the lost Aphrodite of Cnidus by Praxiteles, and how modesty made her cover her private parts with her hand? She seemed inviolate, a true daughter of Plato. But what happens when

Aphrodite comes under threat?' he asked as he projected an image on to the screen. 'Here we have the goddess being molested by the goat-footed Pan, the Greek god of flocks and herds. The statue has been dated to around 100BC. Aphrodite is protecting her privates with her left hand as the old goat hauls on her arm. The goddess has a sandal in her right hand to slap him off, but she doesn't look terrified. Is this because she knows that her protector, Eros, is at her right shoulder, grasping one of Pan's horns? Modesty will prevail, the animal instinct fail. Plato would have approved.'

After the lecture Mackilligin invited Rebecca for a coffee. They sat at a table overlooking the cobbled street because he wasn't worried about being seen occasionally with a student, since he could be giving her guidance about her course.

'I've been thinking about Christmas,' he opened the conversation. 'We should go away.'

'Where to?' she asked, bewildered.

'Away from St Andrews and Edinburgh.'

'How am I going to explain my absence to my parents?'

'You could say that you're visiting a friend you've made at university.'

'I can't, Alan. I've never been away from home at Christmas.'

'There's always a first time.'

'Even if I manage to persuade them to let me go, they'll demand a phone number to check up on me because they'll be suspicious that my friend is male.'

'Can't you say that you have to go in connection with

your studies?' he was almost pleading.

'Where have you in mind?'

'Rome?'

'So I'm to tell them that the art course I'm sitting in on and which doesn't even count towards my degree requires me to go to Rome to look at statues?' she mused. She shook her head. 'Who am I going to say I'm going with? They'll interrogate me and ask for phone numbers. I'm sorry, Alan, the most I can manage are day trips, and even then it's going to be difficult, getting away from my parents. Christmas at home is Mass after Mass, and visiting boring relatives.'

'Then day trips will have to do,' he conceded.

In the following days he spent time on the computer, planning a programme for them both. He was attracted by the festivities in Glasgow and decided that they should spend at least a day there. He would take a hotel room and would stay on there, after putting her on the train back to Edinburgh. The next time Rebecca was in his bed he told her what he had planned, and she said that she would work on her parents as soon as term ended.

He had always liked the approach of the festive season in St Andrews. Early in December the buildings and trees on the historic streets were strung with lights, and families lugged home Christmas trees from the garden centre on South Street. Vivien and he had sat at the windows of cafés, watching the activity, and they had attended parties given by colleagues in substantial houses in Hepburn Gardens. They had gone every year to the carol service in Holy Trinity Church which was packed with hundreds of students, the females in glittering evening dresses, the men in dinner suits or kilts because they were going on to a festive ball.

'This is why this university gets a reputation for having rich students,' Vivien whispered to him. 'Some of these dresses are designer and would cost hundreds of pounds.'

'There are a lot of students who don't come from well-off backgrounds,' Mackilligin had corrected her. 'Scottish lassies who're called Wee Marys because they work hard and live modestly.'

Mackilligin couldn't go with Rebecca to the Holy Trinity carol service because she was singing in the choir. But he went along an hour early before the queue built up, and stood in the dark porch in the chill. He hurried forward when the doors were opened and secured a seat in a pew at the front.

At first he didn't recognise his lover. She had had her hair done and was wearing a sheath-like black evening dress under her red gown as she walked singing 'Once in Royal David's City' down the aisle with the choir to take her place on the altar. He didn't take his eyes off her for the entire service, not even when the minister was delivering suitable festive ponderings from the high elaborately carved pulpit, its pillars and panels made from onyx and alabaster, translucent because of the light within it. Rebecca looked beautiful, holding the folder of carols in both hands, like a figure in an Italian illuminated choir book.

Following the benediction, and having put a twenty pound note in the plate for the collection for charity, Mackilligin lingered at the door, waiting for the choir to come out, so that he could have a word with her.

'You look wonderful,' he complimented her.

'I bought the dress in a charity shop for five pounds. If my mother saw me in it she would die.'

'Are you coming for a drink? We can go to Rufflets Hotel out of town.'

'I'd love to, Alan, but I'm going to the ball.'

He was taken aback.

'You didn't tell me you were going.'

'My friends in the Hall asked me if I wanted to come with them.'

'Come with me and we'll have dinner in Rufflets,' he said desperately.

'I can't, Alan. I've bought a ticket for the ball. If I don't go now I'll miss the bus for the venue.'

He was beside himself with anger as he watched her hurrying, laughing, arms linked with her friends across the road to the waiting bus. She had betrayed him by not telling him she was going to the ball. It made him feel like a perverted old man, hanging about the porch of the church, watching the younger generation running away from him, to their pleasures. He had no part in their lives, and it was as if she had put on the black dress to provoke him.

As he turned up his collar to make his way home through bitter streets he could see her dancing in the arms of a kilted student and then, at the end of the evening, leaving the bus to go home to bed with him in his flat. As soon as he was in the door he made for the whisky bottle, and by the time he estimated that the first dance was being called, he was very drunk.

He was also very angry and searched for his mobile phone, sitting on the sofa, cursing the poor lighting that had been arranged by Vivien as he tried to compose a text message, hitting the wrong keys because they were so small. He was close to throwing the instrument across the room, but held on to it because he had to send a message.

YOU HAVE BETRAYED ME TONIGHT AND I DON'T WANT TO SEE YOU AGAIN.

He watched the small lighted window until it told him: *message sent*, before it went dark. When morning light came through the window whose curtains he had forgotten to close, it took him a minute or so to remember the reason for his drinking. He wanted to go upstairs to sleep off the ferocious hangover, but knew that he had to make amends. He couldn't phone her at the Hall in case it wakened her, so he searched for his mobile so that he could send her a text, making several attempts at getting the message correct because of his trembling hands.

DESPERATELY SORRY FOR CRUEL MESSAGE. PLEASE FORGIVE.

He went upstairs and under a freezing shower, gasping for breath, but knowing that he had to endure it if he were to regain sobriety. When he had dressed he descended to tidy the lounge in case she came round. He sat through the melancholy Monday morning, fixated on the mobile switched on on the table in front of him, but there was no ring to alert him to a message. He had blown it with his jealousy. Of course she would want to go dancing with her own generation. He had no claim on her: she was free to go where she pleased, and to choose her own friends.

At eleven o' clock he could endure it no longer, and picked up his phone to call her. But her mobile invited him to leave a message.

'Apologies from the bottom of my heart. I love you,' he spoke, his voice almost sinking into incoherence with emotion.

After such happiness he couldn't bear the loneliness, as bad as the days following his wife's death. He felt bereaved, abandoned, and in his desperation put on his coat and went out into the winter streets. He should be shopping for himself, but hadn't brought the green hemp bag. He wandered along Market Street, busy with families shopping for Christmas. He wanted to get away from himself, but every step seemed to make his misery worse. He went down a wynd and across North Street, past the initials of the Protestant Patrick Hamilton embedded in the pavement where he had been burned, first martyr of the Reformation. He went under the arch and pushed against the door of St Salvator's Chapel. It yielded and the coldness came to meet him as he went down the aisle, sitting in the pew where he had first heard her playing the organ.

The art historian sat with his face in his hands, asking forgiveness of his lover for his sins of jealousy and possessiveness. He was going to have to get out of St Andrews, to make a new life for himself elsewhere, to learn to live by himself, to expect nothing more from life in the way of companionship. He would go to the personnel office as soon as it opened after the vacation and make arrangements for his retirement.

He had been sitting there for half an hour when the organ struck up, but not sacred music. Someone was playing 'My Love is Like a Red Red Rose'. He ran up the aisle, stumbling on the winding stone staircase up to the organ loft, almost throwing himself on to his lover as she sat on the stool pulling out the stops.

'I thought I'd lost you,' he sobbed, his head against her shoulder.

'You almost did, with that horrible text message,' she rebuked him.

'It was jealousy – jealousy of all those young people in their finery going to the ball, thinking that you would take up with one of them.'

'I enjoyed the dancing, but I came back with my friends from Hall. I saw your text message and thought: I'm not going to reply. If I hadn't come in here to play the organ and seen you looking so pathetic, I wouldn't have contacted you again and that would have been the end of it.'

'Thank God you came here. Let's go back to my house.'

But she put a restraining hand on his arm.

'I don't want to go to bed. I want to do some practice before I go. Go back downstairs and I'll play some festive music for you.'

He went back down to the pew and as he listened to the carols he thought back to the Christmases of his childhood in a modest house on the outskirts of Glasgow, and to the efforts of his parents to make the festive season as joyful as possible. He recalled the care with which his mother had shopped for presents, and the long hours she spent in the kitchen preparing the meals. He remembered his father, the axe raised in his muscular arms as he split wood for the fire that would burn almost continuously from Christmas through to the New Year. Both his parents were dead long since, but the carols on the organ above seemed to restore them to life with a vibrancy that brought tears to their son's eyes.

'I wish you weren't going back to Edinburgh,' he told his lover on the Friday.

'I have to go, or else they'll come to fetch me.'

'But we'll meet in the holidays?' he asked anxiously for confirmation.

'Yes, in Glasgow, but not in Edinburgh. It's too dangerous. What will you do over the vacation?'

'I'll be thinking about you.'

'You must do something more constructive. Try to get on with your book; it's important,' she urged him.

'I'll do that, now I know you've forgiven me for my insane jealousy. What will you do?'

'My mother will have my festive programme mapped out for me, and you can be sure it'll involve shopping and many Masses.'

They crossed the bridge five minutes before the Edinburgh train was due. He was willing that it was delayed, so that he would have more time with her. But the signal was up and it was sliding towards the platform. He carried her luggage aboard and for a moment thought of staying on and accompanying her to Edinburgh. In the course of the day he sent her half a dozen text messages, with the same intimation of constant love. She texted back to confirm that she felt the same, her wish to see him again strengthened by her unhappiness in her own home.

Mackilligin philosophised to himself over a moderate whisky. Because she hadn't lived nearly so long as he had, she lacked experience of life, and couldn't appreciate it from his perspective. No matter how he tried to explain things, she was going to have to live, to make her own mistakes in order to learn about the emotions, and how destructive they could be. In that way she was vulnerable, though she didn't realise it, and was likely to get hurt. She had put her trust in the man who had seduced her, and, he liked to think, who meant more to her than her own father. He hoped she saw him as a warmer human being who wouldn't betray her.

Chapter 8

After he put Rebecca on the train Mackilligin drove home in high spirits. He carried his laptop to his office and resumed work on his book with a zest he hadn't felt for months. He realised fully how fortunate he was that Rebecca hadn't broken off their relationship, and he vowed that he would never send such corrosive text messages again.

He found his ideas flowing and his insight deepening as he tapped away at his laptop in the peace of the Art History building. Several times he stopped to make himself a coffee and to text his lover in Edinburgh. When his inspiration began to falter he closed the laptop and went for a walk along the West Sands. The offshore wind was creating billows, and he found the atmosphere exhilarating. He stopped to watch a dog retrieving a stick from the swell, wondering if he shouldn't get an animal. Apart from the companionship, having to walk it every day would keep him fit.

He turned at the estuary to the river and made his way back through the buffeting wind, the sand lifted in sheets and blown across his path. Instead of going home he went to the coffee shop where Rebecca worked and sat with a cappuccino sprinkled with lethal chocolate dust, thinking fondly of her. Things were going to be different in the future. No more jealousy; no more painful introspection. He had reached a stage in his life when every day had to be regarded as a gift, because time no longer bestowed on him sweeping choices. He had chosen the way, so there was no point in regretting the route that he had taken. Being an art historian had suited his personality, since he was the reflective type. His professorship hadn't been an onerous burden – at least in the early years. Though now there were research exercises and performance measurements, his younger colleagues willingly carried most of these administrative burdens. He had ample time to study surviving sculptures of the Hellenistic world at his light-box, or in art galleries and museums, and he received grants to subsidise his research. He was also invited to universities abroad to lecture on his subject, and had been four times to Athens, the last to receive an honorary degree.

He knew that he had had a privileged life, especially in his career. The loss of Vivien had been cruel, but then again, they had lived in harmony for many years, sharing an aesthetic vision. So many talented people died before they realised their gifts. He thought of the artists, musicians and writers, some still in their mothers' arms, who had been pushed with guns into the gas chambers. He was fortunate to have lived as long as he had, fortunate to have had such a fulfilling career and to have been to so many places, cruising on the Aegean with Vivien, lecturing his fellow-travellers by day and making love in the humid nights below an open porthole.

He had booked a room in the Millennium Hotel, George Square, Glasgow, for three nights of the festive season, not because he didn't want to be alone in St Andrews, but because Rebecca was coming through from Edinburgh to see him on the twenty third. When he met her off the train in the adjacent station he practically lifted her out of her shoes with his embrace.

'How did you manage to get away?' he enquired.

'By telling them I was going to the house of a university friend for the day to discuss a theology essay I have to write over the holidays. I said it was about the Book of Revelation.'

They had coffee in the glass-walled lounge overlooking the Square, festive lights strung above the sombre statuary of civic fathers and empire builders. A temporary ice rink had been laid in the Square.

'We'll try some skating later,' he told his lover.

He had never rushed matters in his life. He hadn't pursued scholarship, in the way that academics had to do now, publishing books and papers as fast as they could churn them out in order to get a personal chair. Even in his marriage he had practised a steady pace that suited both their artistic interests and ambitions. Before he could start writing a book about classical sculpture he had had to devote years of study to its products, and Vivien wouldn't begin the design for a stained glass window without long pondering.

But in his relationship with Rebecca he hadn't been so cautious. He had pushed things (perhaps, he thought, on account of his age, and the awareness that time was becoming severely limited), wanting to get her into bed as soon as possible, then becoming jealous of rivalry from the males of her own generation. His impulsive pursuit had almost destroyed their relationship, and he knew that he had to be much more laid back in the future, which was why, though he was desperate to go upstairs with this attractive young woman, he poured them more coffee and listened to her account of her stultifying home life in the Edinburgh suburban villa, where, she told him, her mother was in terror of what the neighbours would think; where, in summer, the grass couldn't be allowed to grow beyond a week; where the autumn leaves were suctioned up and bagged, not burned, because a bonfire (though permissible at certain hours) would have irritated the neighbours.

This was why he found it easy to listen to his lover and be amused by her account of her mother's addiction to shopping, wardrobe rails packed with clothes, yards of shoes.

'But how can they afford it?' he speculated. 'Your father's only a teacher and your mother doesn't work.'

'She had a wealthy father, and her income from her investments is bigger than my father's salary. She seems to think that she has to spend it all each year, or it'll stop coming.'

'But she's generous to you.'

'If kitting out your daughter in clothes that belong on a much older woman – the word I'm looking for is frump – is your idea of generosity, it isn't mine. I call it an imposition and a waste. That's why I have to earn money for myself.'

But he didn't want to get into a discussion on her employment in the coffee shop in St Andrews, because the old hackles of jealousy might arise and spoil this most pleasant reunion. He was happier than he had been for a very long time. The winter sun was streaming through the window, lighting up a face that seemed to get even more beautiful every time he saw it. Beyond the window, in the Square, was the bustle of life, parents out shopping with their children, a bright crowd that reminded him of a Renoir painting. Life was good, was a blessing. The age gap between them seemed to have shrunk, the coffee and the little plate of shortbread had been tasty. It was time to go upstairs.

On the phone he had asked for a room overlooking the Square because he remembered its elegance from his boyhood. He had come this way shopping with his mother, when she wasn't on duty in the Infirmary as a nursing sister. She was a cool headed, competent woman, who seemed to carry – metaphorically speaking – a thermometer above her heart and which she consulted when her husband's temperature (temper) began to rise. A kiss on his cheek was the sedative she administered, and that calmed him. He had had the ability to go to university, but family poverty prohibited this. He had become an insurance clerk, his bowler and black coat belying the modesty of his salary, with his wife earning more as a nurse. But he did have an appreciation of music, and sat in the evening with his habitual packet of cigarettes, listening to symphonies - Sibelius was his favourite composer - on the glistening black disks which he handled so carefully as he slipped them in and out of their brown sleeves. He took his son on the tram to the Kelvingrove Art Gallery on a Saturday morning, and as they stood in front of the paintings he explained to the boy (bored at the beginning; he would rather have been playing with his friends) about perspective. He also bought his son - there was a sister, but she wasn't so indulged - a wooden box containing a selection of tubes of paints, but when Alan took his effort to his father for critical evaluation there were no more purchases of art materials, though the excursions to the art galleries continued, and included train journeys through to Edinburgh.

He had read fine art at Edinburgh University because of his father's encouragement. When it was the son's turn to do the educating, he shared his books in the vacations with the elderly man, pointing out aspects of style and perspective which his father had omitted during his tuition of his son. His mother was always a benign presence in the background, displaying the same calm she showed in the wards when a patient sensed - without being told by the consultant - that he or she was going to die. The little inverted watch she wore at her starched bust became, to her son, a symbol of her control over chaos, even in the home, when her husband, now retired from the tedium of the insurance office, grew embittered at the waste of his life at a desk, when he could have been an art historian like his son.

Mackilligin was recalling his upbringing as he sat with Rebecca in the sun-filled lounge of the hotel overlooking George Square. He had been blessed with caring parents, as he had been blessed with a caring wife, and now, late in life when most widowers were alone, a youthful lover.

It seemed the appropriate moment to go up in the elevator, to close the curtains in the superior room, to fold back the bed cover. He took care to be gentle and considerate, but he sensed that his partner needed this physical relief after the oppressive Edinburgh house. They lay recovering the calm level of their breathing in the quiet room, its double glazing excluding the traffic and the voices from the Square, where the ice rink was being prepared for the evening. It was one of these times he felt that silence was preferable. But it wasn't the studied silence of standing in front of a sculpture. It was the silence of satisfaction and fulfilment, the realisation that love didn't require vocalism, but could be conveyed by the touch of a hand, the turn of a head, a smile.

In fact Mackilligin was so relaxed that he fell asleep and was soon snoring. This amused his lover as she lay beside him. The noise showed his vulnerability. Since he was in such deep repose, she had the opportunity to study his face turned towards her on the pillow. She watched the lips pursing and reforming as he blew out his fatigue, like the four swollen-cheeked cherubs she had seen, sitting in the corners of the cornice, puffing out the four points of the compass in a Midlothian stately home her school class had toured. Very lightly with her fingertips she touched the folded skin under his closed eyes, as if she could smooth it out. The brow was high and untroubled in this dreamless sleep of satisfaction. The hair (she had several strands between her fingers) was grey, of fine texture, and there was a bare circle at the crown, the skin mottled by summers of sun on Iona.

He was endearing because he was vulnerable, she

decided. But he was also old and that frightened her. She remembered her maternal grandmother after her stroke, lying with twisted mouth, helpless. Could this happen to the man lying beside her in the dimmed hotel room, Rebecca asked herself apprehensively? Would it be her fault because her younger body demanded vigorous sex? How could she cope? Would she do what her mother had done? Instead of taking the stroke victim into her home (though there was a spare bedroom and money to pay for private nursing), she had put her mother into a nursing home, and only visited once a month. Would she, Rebecca, still a comparatively young woman, be standing in a nursing home beside the bed of this man in such a deep sleep lying beside her?

As she lay in the Glasgow hotel bed she saw herself going down a long hospital corridor with a bunch of flowers in cellophane, to her lover lying helpless in bed, having to be assisted at every movement by nursing staff, his penis inserted into the bed bottle. Would there be someone of her own age in her life, or would she be condemned to celibacy and sacrifice until the art historian died? Oh God, what had she got herself into, she asked herself?

But before these sombre fears could develop into panic, the subject of her silent soliloquy wakened.

'How long have I been asleep?'

'Fifteen minutes.'

But it was twice that.

He felt refreshed and suggested lunch. They went to a restaurant in the Merchant City where the furniture was of rustic design, carved with a chain-saw, the table they sat at a slab of oak, the bark still on it. The place was crowded with office parties in paper hats, wine bottles in clusters in silver buckets with the sheen of the ice within on them.

'I'm going to have the vegetarian haggis,' Rebecca told the waiter.

'I've never tried that,' her dining companion admitted.

'You should. It's very tasty – and much better for your health than meat.'

'Are you a vegetarian?' he asked in surprise, having served her meat without protest.

'When there's a choice, though there isn't one at home. I have two dedicated carnivores as parents.'

'You should have told me, Rebecca,' he said mournfully.

'It doesn't matter. Two vegetarian haggis,' she instructed.

He enjoyed its nutty texture, and the Chianti encased in wicker he had ordered to go with it. Intimate conversation became difficult because the noise the office workers were making increased with their consumption of alcohol. He saw a surreptitious dangling hand deftly fondling the cleft between buttocks and not being lifted away.

'I'd like to go to St Andrew's Cathedral,' Rebecca informed him.

'Where is it?' this son of a staunch Protestant enquired.

'I've a map,' she told him, reaching down for her handbag.

He took her hand on the crowded pavement. She paused at plate glass windows displaying designer clothes for the younger person.

'Come in and choose your Christmas present,' he offered.

'I couldn't possibly let you pay these prices.'

'Christmas isn't about economy. Come on.'

He sat while she tried on a long-sleeved top that looked to him like a rugby jersey.

'I like this one.'

He tried to conceal his surprise at the sum of seventy pounds on the machine which the assistant handed him to press his PIN number into.

When they entered St Andrew's Cathedral on the waterfront Rebecca sat in silence in a pew at the back. He didn't know if his lover was praying or resting, but he was content to sit beside her in silence, giving thanks for his happiness. Though Mackilligin had been sent to Sunday School, his father was sceptical about the concept of a god, and his mother had seen too much suffering in the Infirmary to be convinced. Rebecca touched his arm and he followed her out of the Cathedral. They went back to the hotel for another session in bed, and when the festive lights were brightening above George Square they shared a bath, its soapy fragrance spilling over the sides to their hilarity.

'Have you ever skated?' he enquired as they went down in the lift.

'It's not on my father's list of sports. He says it's a form of dancing and that most of the males are gay.'

'I'll teach you,' he offered.

He hired two sets of skates and knelt to lace up her boots before putting on his own. As a boy he had gone skating at the Crossmyloof Rink and was told by the coach that he had a 'good style.'

He led Rebecca by the hand on to the rink which was

already busy. She was wobbling on the blades, but he taught her simple manoeuvres, and as she was about to fall, he saved her in his arms. He was exhilarated, his breath mingling visibly with hers as they moved together on hissing blades under an angel whose wings, shimmering with light, seemed to give it the motive power to ascend into the dark urban firmament. He left Rebecca clinging to the barrier as he wove among the skaters. When he returned with a gloveful of roasted chestnuts he saw her watching a skater. The youth was wearing a reversed baseball cap, his denims rolled up to his knees, travelling at speed round the perimeter, then weaving among the others on the ice as if about to collide with them, but avoiding them at the last second, going on to more impressive gyrations, leaping, turning in the air, the epitome of grace and daring. He was young, he was fearless, and, stationary at the barrier with his gloved palm of cooling chestnuts, the elderly art historian saw his lover watching the exhibitionist with profound admiration. It was as if the lights had suddenly gone out and Mackilligin was left in darkness in the centre of the ice, alone, not knowing which direction to take, or where the obstacles lay, whereas this youth, in all his arrogance and poise, was performing in the light, and had the advantage of time, of stamina, of optimism ahead of him. As he waltzed the concepts of ageing, of physical frailty, were beyond his ken.

Bearing the cooling chestnuts, Mackilligin knew that the skater, who was now doing figures of eight in front of Rebecca, should be the one to lead her on to the ice by the hand, to teach her to skate, and then to take her up to a room, to fire her body with urgency and stamina. For one foolish moment he wanted to throw the chestnuts at the prancing skater, or – more foolish still – to launch himself on to the ice and challenge him to a contest of skill. But he knew which one would win, which one had the technique, the thrust in his legs, the sheer speed, the confidence.

Instead, feeling his age as he had never felt it before, he skated slowly along the barrier to Rebecca and offered her the chestnuts.

'He's wonderful, isn't he?' she enthused as the skater wove in and out of the beginners, outpacing the experienced.

As the youthful exhibitionist passed he reached across and, without losing momentum or balance, snatched a chestnut from Mackilligin's palm and popped it into his mouth, winking at Rebecca. In his impotent fury her lover dropped the rest, scattering round his inert skates.

Chapter 9

The prospect of staying in the Glasgow hotel ov[er] season no longer appealed to Mackilligin, so he [took] the room he had already paid for and headed hom[e to] St Andrews, though his house there had too many sombre associations of happy Christmases with his late wife, and though he knew it would feel lonely without Rebecca. He went to the Christmas Eve carol service for university staff and friends in the small exquisite St Leonard's Chapel, where a porter went round with a step ladder and a taper to light the candles. He sat in the pew that he had always sat in with his wife, the carols backed by the organ in the gallery above bringing tears of recollection to him.

'How are you?' Fenwick the anatomist from the medical school greeted him with a firm handshake when they were drinking mulled wine in the outer room.

'I'm fine, David.'

'Come and see us at New Year. We keep open house.'

He thanked him for the invitation, but knew that he wouldn't go. It had started to snow while the carol service was in progress, and as Mackilligin walked home the lit shop windows reflected on the white street reminded him of the Christmas cards his family had received when he was a boy. In a restaurant a couple were sitting in the window table and the art historian, snow mantling his shoulders, stood to watch as the young man leaned over to touch his companion's face. As her eyes sparkled in the candle between them, Mackilligin experienced the helpless ɑn he had with the skater

ɦimself as a young man,

gh restaurant. But he also

ind the plate glass window

ɨ of his bereavement, the art

ɨ cold desolate place without

students. St Salvator's Chapel

where ʒ.. ɪn was darkened and grim, its
stained glass windowʒ .ɪe slabs of lead. The students
considered it unlucky to stand on the initials of Patrick
Hamilton inset in the cobbles, where the Protestant had
been martyred by fire, but Mackilligin left his footprint in
the snow on the site of anguish.

On Christmas Day, instead of consuming turkey by
himself in one of St Andrews's smart hotels, even though
he would be surrounded by revellers in paper hats hauling
at crackers, he had bought himself a breast of chicken. He
had also purchased an individual Christmas pudding which
he had with a small carton of cream, something that his late
wife prohibited because of the danger to his arteries. He ate
on the sofa where he had began the seduction of Rebecca,
and as he thought wistfully about what she would be doing
that day, he made serious inroads into the bottle of wine,
then started on whisky.

Would she phone? That was the question which
preoccupied him that dreary day as he flicked through the
television channels in search of something that would take
up his attention, moving rapidly on from the serious face of

the monarch, commiserating with her subjects in a world made tense by terrorism and anxious over making ends meet. But he wasn't into economics and politics. He voted Scottish Nationalist from a patriotic feeling, not because he had investigated and compared the policies of the various Scottish parties. Nor did he watch much television, apart from the programmes on art on BBC4.

By four o' clock he was drunk, staring at the mobile on the table in front of him as if trying to turn on some psychic power that would make it ring from Edinburgh. Why the hell was she not phoning? The jealousy and truculence that he thought he had controlled were returning, fuelled by drink. It had been a mistake, having wine with his solitary festive meal, but the damage was done: the alcohol was in his system, acting both as an anaesthetic (blotting out memories of Christmas Days with his late wife) and as an irritant, making him impatient for a message.

Christmas lunch was always late in the Campbell-Arthurson house in Morningside, because the family went to Mass, after which the chatelaine insisted on her husband and daughter sitting round the television and savouring the monarch's message as an aperitif.

'Isn't she remarkable for her age?' Felicity enthused. 'And it's such a beautiful dress. Of course she has her own dress advisor. But she does suit light blue, and her hair is most beautifully coiffured.'

Her daughter wanted to laugh at this quaint phrase, but it was too dangerous, so she sat, looking at, but not listening to the plasma screen her father had bought so that he could get the widest possible perspective on sporting occasions. The screen was fixed to the wall and was stared at reverentially by the couple as though it were an old master. As for Rebecca, she wanted to giggle at the way the screen flattened out the Queen to make her look small and stout, like a figure in a cartoon.

There was no hurry in this elegant house on Christmas Day. The turkey, well larded in foil, was cooking on a timer which would sound like the bell from the Mass altar when the meal – including roast potatoes lubricated with goose grease – was ready. The mahogany table had been set with the King's Pattern silver plated cutlery, the blue Wedgwood set, the Georgian candle-sticks that Felicity had inherited from her father, a gift from a grateful client. There was a Christmas tree in the lounge, but it was artificial, and its branches, guaranteed not to shed the plastic needles, could be folded up and boxed for the attic until the following year. The presents were under the tree. The labrador sprawled on the sheepskin rug.

When the royal address was finished the turkey was slid from the oven and carved by the rugby referee while his wife arranged breasts and legs on the blue plates. It was the tradition since the age of five that Rebecca say the Latin grace, but as she bowed her head to give thanks for the Christmas dinner, she was thinking that this year was different from those that had gone before. She had shorn her hair in opposition to her parents; she had a wardrobe of the gear of her own generation in St Andrews; and she had a lover. As she said 'Amen' she raised her face and saw her mother's still bowed head adding a codicil to her prayer. *If you only knew*, her daughter thought with satisfaction as well as guilt.

Her father didn't speak as he was eating. He was too busy packing in the nutrition that would give him the energy to pound the pavements every morning before the suburb had awakened, thinking of the baseball game beamed from the States which he would pick up later on a satellite channel, even though the two females in his house might want to watch something else, like the weepie black and white films his wife was addicted to.

Rebecca's present from her parents was always something useful – this year thermal underwear for the rigours of St Andrews. She gave her father an old book on cricket which she had found in an antiquarian shop in St Andrews. For her mother she had bought fragrant soap; always safe.

At five o' clock when her father had the remote control in his hand and was searching for sport in bleak December, and her mother was in the kitchen, stacking the dish washer, Rebecca went up to her room, locked the door and phoned her lover on the prohibited mobile he had given her. She thanked him for his Christmas present of a silver Cross pen inscribed with her name.

'Are you drunk?' she asked.

'No, just sleepy.'

He told her with great affection how much he was missing her and how he wished they were lying together in his bed in St Andrews. She heard music in the background and wondered momentarily if he were holding a party, but she knew that he was too anti-social. He hoped that she saw it as the solitary Christmas of a lonely man, who had got drunk because – as he kept telling her, and she had no reason to disbelieve him – he was missing her so much. He thanked her profusely for the art book she had left on his sofa, with a post-it stuck to it, warning: 'not to be opened until Christmas.' He told her that the illustrations in it – supreme statues of the classical world - were 'magnificent.'

When she heard her mother on the stairs Rebecca terminated the call swiftly with 'I love you.' That was all that he wanted to hear. He required no more whisky, no more food, but instead made his way up to his bed, using both hands on the wall for support and guidance, as if he had never been in the house before. He fell on the bed and slept dreamlessly, deeply, still in his clothes.

After the alcoholic excesses of Christmas he had a quiet new year at home. He watched an art programme on Tintoretto which he had recorded, and instead of waiting for the bells, went up to bed, knowing that Rebecca would be doing the same, since her parents didn't see in Hogmanay. If a first footer had arrived at their door with the traditional gifts of a bottle of whisky and a lump of coal, he or she wouldn't be admitted.

He met his lover at Leuchars Station, embracing her on the platform, among the hordes of returning students. She dumped her luggage in McIntosh Hall before hurrying along to his house and leading him by the hand up the stairs to bed. In the cathartic peace after their coupling she explained that her Christmas had been as boring as always, and that she couldn't bear the thought of another in that house.

'It's a long time away. Anything might happen,' he cautioned her.

He wasn't thinking of her but of his own mortality, a theme that had been tormenting him again in his isolation over the festive season. His body was warning him that he was ageing, that the pains he felt when his feet found the floor in the morning were arthritic, perhaps because he had lived beside the sea for so long, in a town notorious for its haars, when the streets seemed to be filled with smoke, as they must have been in the bonfires of the Reformation at the Cathedral. When he went to relieve himself in the porcelain orifice he knew that the delay in starting the stream must be related to the condition of his prostate which was probably fraying like an old electric cable. He feared that soon his member wouldn't rise to the occasion, whereas the body stretched out beside him was young, the skin without blemish, the breasts self-supporting, the nipples erect. The pronounced pubic bone was a feature of her body he found hugely erotic.

What would happen if he couldn't get it up? He knew it was a crude thought, but he wasn't going to share it with anybody, and besides, there was no other way of describing it. The flowery language, the superlatives, were reserved for the young Adonis, his scrotum tight, the penis responsive to the slightest touch of another hand. He had had these attributes, once, but they were going. What could he do about it? Become one of those sad elderly men who went online to look for potions that would increase potency, on offer from overseas pharmacies at outrageous prices, inclusive of being couriered to your door? He already received a torrent of spam, offering him something to 'increase your penis by inches.' Did a man past sixty really need the extra length – and girth?

He had been silent for a considerable time, and his lover beside him, luxuriating in the fire that was still in her receptive loins, asked him what he was thinking.

'About you,' he lied.

'What about me?' she teased.

'How glad I am that you're back.'

'You're a romantic, Alan, but I suppose all art historians are. I've often wondered: do they get a kick out of looking at the paintings of naked ladies?'

'That depends who the artist is. Renoir's *Nude in the Sun*, with her hand over her vagina – yes. But Picasso? You have to search for the organ in question and may find it in her armpit. Artists want the observers of their paintings of naked flesh to find it erotic.'

'I'd like to have a try at stained glass,' she told him.

'Really? What's prompted this?'

'I suppose the beautiful windows in St Salvator's Chapel.'

'As you know there's my wife's studio here, with the books she used to learn from. There's a woman who lives in a house by the harbour who's also a stained glass artist. Vivien knew and admired her, and they collaborated on at least one window. Would you like me to speak to her about giving you lessons?'

'Yes, but I'm going to pay for them myself.'

'Let's see what she says. Are you going back to working in the coffee shop?'

'I need the money and I like the work. It's relaxing after studying.'

He knew better than to make an issue of this again, after such a blissful evening. He didn't sleep straight away, despite his earlier exertions. He left the muted bedside lamp on as he stretched out naked, hands behind his head, intrigued by the thought that, like his late wife, his lover was interested in stained glass artistry. The spiritualists would claim that Vivien was working from beyond the grave to make the widower and his new love compatible, but he didn't believe this. Whatever the reason, it was satisfying to think that someone would be using her studio.

The following afternoon, after his seminar, he went along to the house by the harbour where the stained glass artist resided. It was a historic property with crow-stepped gables and a red tiled roof. Jessica Rae took him up to a window overlooking the sea, pieces of glass spread out on her worktable.

'This view is my inspiration,' she told him as she lifted a sleeping cat to offer her visitor its chair. 'In the summer I often see dolphins passing, leaping out of the water, as if they're greeting me. It was so sad about Vivien. She was such a gifted artist and such a fine person, I so miss her visits. Did you know that we hoped to collaborate on another project?'

'I didn't,' he confessed.

'Oh yes, it was for a private house.'

Before the grey haired Englishwoman who was in her seventies could elaborate on a design that would never be executed, he told her the reason for his visit.

'And this student has never done any stained glass work before?' she questioned him cautiously.

'No, but she's artistic, and I'm sure she'll pick it up.'

This woman of independent spirit had come to St Andrews half a century before to study, and, like so many of her kind, had found it impossible to leave after graduating. At the beginning she had supplemented her private income with tuition, until she began to attract significant and lucrative commissions. He wondered at the lack of spectacles, the steady hands.

'Tell her to come and see me at two o'clock on Wednesday afternoon, which I know is the university's recreation time,' she told him, as precise in her choice of words as she was meticulous in her choice of colours for the appealing frameworks of lead which she created.

He was in his office the following day when the secretary came in to tell him that he had a visitor, a Mrs Campbell-Arthurson.

'Tell her I've gone out,' he panicked.

'I'm sorry, Alan, but I've already said that you're in.'

He could have told his caller that he had a student with him, but he knew that she would stay until he was free. Was this to be a showdown, accusing him of seducing her daughter? But the only person who could have told her was

Rebecca.

They shook hands formally and sat at the table he used for seminars.

'I'm sorry to disturb you like this, professor, but I'm worried about Rebecca.'

'In what way?' he asked cautiously, selecting his words carefully as if he were preparing a monograph on a sculptor.

'She's changed so much since she's come to St Andrews.'

'I only see her a couple of times a week, when she sits in on my lectures, but I haven't noticed any changes,' he informed her evasively.

'Her hair is different and she's wearing denims.'

'I'm not in the habit of studying my students' hair, and most of them wear denims – including members of staff.'

'She had such beautiful long hair, and she wore modest clothes. Now she looks like these awful young women I see slouching along Princes Street in denims, with the tops of their buttocks showing.'

'It's the style of the young, I'm afraid, Mrs Campbell-Arthurson.'

'Felicity please.'

'Felicity,' he repeated reluctantly, without returning the first name invitation.

'And her personality has changed.'

'I wouldn't really know about that. She speaks to me from time to time after a lecture, to ask a question, and that's the only contact I have with her.'

'I wonder if a man's involved?'

He felt his muscles tensing. Was this well-dressed woman

from an affluent area of Edinburgh shrewder than he had given her credit for? Did she suspect that he was having an affair with her daughter?

'You mean: does she have a boyfriend? Why would I know that? When we talk, it's about art, not her personal circumstances. Many students have relationships; it's part of being at university.'

'She was such a pretty child, and always so obedient,' her mother recalled wistfully. 'Wherever we took her on holiday – and we went abroad most summers so that she could see the great places of civilization, like Rome – she was admired for her clothes and her manners. The truth is, Professor Mackilligin, I didn't want her to come to St Andrews.'

'You mean: you wanted her to go to Edinburgh, to live at home.'

'Yes.'

'Why?'

'Why?' she repeated, taken aback by the truculence of his tone. 'Because I wanted my only child to live under my care. It was her father who wanted her to study classics at his alma mater.'

'Surely it's good for young people to get away from home,' he persisted. 'What would you have wanted her to study at Edinburgh?'

'I wanted Rebecca to become a nun, because she seemed to me to have the serene personality that's required, professor. She could have gone to Edinburgh University to study theology, and then entered a convent.'

'Is that what Rebecca wants, Felicity?'

'What does that matter now, since she's changed so much? She speaks very disrespectfully to her father and myself, and she slouches about the house in denims and tops without a bra. She's a different girl since she came to St Andrews, professor. Christmas was very difficult. I had neighbours in for coffee on Boxing Day and she was really morose towards them. She gave us the impression that she didn't want to be with us, though we believe we've provided her with a happy stable home. It seems to us that she's become very secretive.'

'What age is she?' he asked, though he knew already.

'She'll be nineteen in a few months' time, far too young to know her own mind. I'm sorry for bothering you with my worries.'

'She's legally an adult, Felicity, and the university treats her as such. Staff have no power to interfere between her and her parents.'

'But she respects and trusts you, professor, and that's very important to my husband and myself. If you notice anything untoward, will you get in touch with us?' She opened the gilt clasps of her handbag, took out a black notebook, extracted a gold pencil from the spine and wrote on a page which she passed across to him.

'That's our number in Edinburgh. We'll be so grateful if you would keep an eye on her. If you hear that she's getting into bad company, please let us know. And please don't tell Rebecca that I was here; I'm going back on the next train.'

While she was speaking he had kept his hands under the table because they were trembling, and after she had gone he wanted a drink, and went to the cupboard where he kept a whisky bottle for favoured callers. He knew that he couldn't tell Rebecca about his visitor and report their conversation because she would go on the phone to berate her mother, and God knows what would come out. As he drank his substantial whisky he was still wondering if his visitor was suspicious of him.

Chapter 10

Mackilligin got drunk that night after Felicity Campbell-Arthurson's visit, out of a sense of self-loathing as well as fear. She had put her trust in him to look after Rebecca's moral welfare at St Andrews, yet he had already seduced her daughter. At the same time he couldn't be sure that she wasn't suspicious that he had designs on her daughter, because Rebecca had warned him that she was a cunning manipulative woman. Wasn't it time to bring the affair to an end?

But as he unscrewed the cap of the whisky bottle again he knew that he couldn't stop, for two reasons. Rebecca would ask him why he was breaking it off, and since he couldn't tell her about the visit of her mother, she would assume that he had tired of her. But he sensed that she wouldn't agree to a parting, and could accuse him of exploiting his position as her teacher. The second reason was that he was in love with her and couldn't let her go, which is why he put away the whisky bottle and went to bed.

But there was another problem that kept him from sleeping, despite the amount of liquor he had consumed. Rebecca seemed to get more and more attractive, perhaps because he had helped her to mature, and therefore there was the even stronger possibility that a student of her own age would make a play for her. She seemed to be especially vulnerable in January, after the exams, because there was a break before teaching resumed. She wasn't going home to Edinburgh, and a number of male students were still in town.

He decided to take her to Iona, not only to remove her from temptation, but because he wanted to go back for old times' sake. Winter certainly wasn't the best time to go to the island, but on the other hand his sister-in-law Charlotte, who jointly owned the family holiday house with Vivien, only went in summer. He could have phoned her and told her that he wanted to use the house for a short stay, but sleeping in it with Rebecca would have been a betrayal of Vivien, and the special times they had had on Iona, so he decided to book two single rooms in one of the hotels because he was known on Iona.

When he put his proposal to Rebecca on the night after her mother had visited him she was enthusiastic.

'I've always wanted to go to Iona.'

'It's not the best time to see the island,' he cautioned. 'But at least it isn't overrun with tourists, as it is at Easter and in the summer.'

'What am I going to tell my mother?'

'Why do you need to tell her anything?'

'She might phone Hall to check up on me.'

'Phone her the night before we leave and tell her that you're going to be working late in the library for the next few days, writing an essay.'

Mackilligin drove to Oban and took the car ferry across to the island of Mull. It was a blustery day, but Rebecca stayed out on deck, wrapped up in a thermal jacket that had belonged to Vivien, throwing bread to the seabirds that swooped to snatch the offerings from the waves. They drove through the glens of Mull, seeing hungry deer that had descended from the bens, and torrents spilling down the hillsides. They left the car at the ferry port and crossed the narrow sound to Iona, trundling their suitcases on wheels along the charming street to the hotel.

'This is wonderful,' Rebecca enthused as they sat in the lounge, drinking tea as they looked out across the sound.

'Beautiful but dangerous,' he remarked.

'What do you mean?'

'I read in the Irish Annals that the whole community of monks drowned, presumably when their boat capsized in heavy seas. And in bad weather the ferry might not be able to make the crossing for several days.'

'I'd like to be marooned on this island,' she said.

'I'm going to take you to show you something that will interest you,' he told her the following morning.

They went along to the cathedral, and he arranged two chairs beneath the stained glass figure of St Margaret of Scotland. He watched Rebecca's face which wasn't lit up by the winter sun streaming through the window and laying a coloured mosaic on the flagstones at her feet, but with an illumination that seemed to come from within her, as if she had found her vocation in life, in the same way as his late wife had when she sat in front of the same window as a child, barefooted, her hair dripping after her swim.

He felt a hand on his shoulder and when he turned he saw Vivien's sister standing in a long waxed coat and matching wide-brimmed hat.

'What are you doing here, Alan?'

He was so taken aback that he almost knocked over his chair as he stood up to kiss her.

'Research.'

'Are you only here for the day?'

He knew that it was too dangerous to lie, so he told her that it was a three day visit, and that he was staying at the hotel. But how was he going to introduce Rebecca, who was still sitting, as if mesmerised by the stained glass window? Could he pretend that she was someone he had just met in the cathedral, and with whom he was sharing his appreciation of the window? But if Rebecca overheard him, she would probably get up and challenge his introduction.

'This is Rebecca, one of my students.'

He didn't give her second name, because Charlotte lived in Edinburgh and might know it. He saw, the way that his sister-in-law extended her hand, that she was suspicious.

'You should have let me know you were coming, and I could have got two rooms ready.'

Was this meant to be sarcastic? It was one of these awkward moments, rare in his life, when he didn't know what to do. He could see the cynicism and anger in Charlotte's face that he had chosen to take up with a woman who could be his daughter, when Vivien wasn't a year dead.

'You don't come at this time of year,' he pointed out, buying time.

'I'm here to get the house ready to sell.'

'To sell?' he said, surprised.

'It's hardly used now, and it's getting damp. My children loved Iona when they were young, but now they find the island too quiet, and would rather go abroad with their friends. Besides, I need the money to help out my grandchildren with their university fees, so they're not saddled with debts for the rest of their lives. Morag is going to Edinburgh this year to study medicine, and Rory has a place for classics at Cambridge.'

He knew that it was the wrong place to conduct a conversation about the ownership of the holiday house, though half of it had been willed to Vivien. Charlotte must be assuming that he had no entitlement to inherit Vivien's half, and therefore she was going ahead with the sale without consulting him. Not that he wanted the money, but he felt that she had been devious. He had never liked her. She wasn't artistic and sensitive like her sister, but had been trained as a lawyer.

'I want to get the house on the market for Easter,' she explained.

They stood about, awkwardly, but Charlotte wasn't going to let him go.

'You must both come to supper tonight.'

'We don't want to put you to any trouble,' he told her.

'No, no, I insist – for one final family meal in the old island homestead.'

'Is Alex with you?' he asked.

Her husband was a mild-mannered man, a chartered accountant.

'No, he's too busy. I came up by myself, with a load of emulsion and paint in the boot of the car to do some decorating, to hide some of the blemishes. Shall we say seven?'

He nodded in meek acquiescence, and in the glance the formidable woman gave to Rebecca before she turned away he saw dislike.

'It's the first time I've seen you lost for words,' his lover observed.

'I don't like my sister-in-law. I've never liked her.'

'She certainly didn't like me. She knows we have a relationship.'

'It's none of her bloody business,' he said heatedly.

'Then why didn't you turn down the invitation?'

He didn't want to get into an argument with Rebecca in the cathedral, where words became amplified, and heads turned disapprovingly at the breaking of the pious silence.

'I don't want to make an enemy of her,' was his weak excuse.

'Why, what damage can she do to you?'

'I don't want her going spreading the story in Edinburgh that her brother-in-law is having an affair with a student. It's not that I'm ashamed of it,' he added hastily, 'but you never know, it could get back to your parents.'

'Does she know my parents?'

'I don't know, but we shouldn't take a chance on it. If they knew that we were staying together on Iona they wouldn't think it was an innocent pilgrimage.'

They made their way along the road to the holiday house, with a torch borrowed from the hotel. The house smelt of emulsion as they were ushered into the sparking fire of driftwood in the sitting-room and offered drinks. He knew that he had to watch his consumption of alcohol in case he said the wrong thing. Rebecca took a small sherry and sat with the glass balanced on her knee.

'You must have many happy memories of this house,' Charlotte began.

It was a cunning, cruel opener to show his young companion that he had had a contented and fulfilled life with her sister Vivien long before he met her.

'I enjoyed coming in the summer,' he admitted.

'How many years was it you were married?'

'Thirty seven.'

'You honeymooned here, if you remember,' the persistent attempt to exclude Rebecca from the larger part of his life continued.

'We did. But of course we came as students, when your parents were alive.'

'Ah, those summers,' Charlotte said with a sigh that seemed to be genuine regret. 'I was looking at the dinghy this afternoon, wondering if I could sell it with the house, but it's rotten because it wasn't maintained after daddy died. He liked to keep everything in order.'

'He was a minister,' he informed Rebecca.

'A very good man,' his daughter added.

'No doubt about that,' he concurred.

'Excuse me,' she said, and went out.

He reached across and squeezed Rebecca's hand in support.

'Remember this?' Charlotte asked, opening the box and lifting out the melodeon.

'We had some wonderful ceilidhs with your father playing,' he reminisced. 'He was brilliant at Scottish tunes.'

'He loved the old melodies, like Burns's songs. Do you play an instrument, Rebecca?'

'I play the organ.'

'She's an excellent organist,' he came in. 'She plays in St Salvator's Chapel.'

'That must be very fulfilling. What are you studying?'

'Classics and theology.'

'Oh, I thought you were one of Alan's art history students.'

'I am, but only part-time. I sit in on one of his classes.'

It was a piece of information that he wished Rebecca hadn't imparted, but on the other hand he could see that she was going to stand up for herself against his sister-in-law, as she had stood up against her parents, and that he was responsible for her recently found confidence.

'And are you studying art on Iona?'

'Rebecca is interested in working in stained glass, and I wanted her to see the St Margaret window in the Abbey.'

'I presume you still have Vivien's studio.'

'It's intact,' he informed Charlotte. 'I haven't touched it since her death.'

'That's very convenient. Where are you staying in St Andrews, Rebecca?'

The question implied that it was with him.

'In McIntosh Hall.'

'And is it comfortable?'

'Yes, it is.'

'Good. I must go and see to the supper.'

They could see her silhouette at the stove through the lighted glass door.

'She's determined to give us a hard time,' Rebecca complained.

'You're holding your own. I'm proud of you.'

She stood up and lifted a photograph from the mantelpiece.

'Is this you and your wife?'

He knew that Charlotte had put it there deliberately, to embarrass him.

'Yes it is, taken on the beach below the house.'

'She's very pretty.'

'She was,' he confirmed, trying to keep his voice subdued, not only because of the woman in the kitchen, but also because he didn't want Rebecca to compare herself to her predecessor.

'You both look very happy.'

'It's easy to be happy on Iona,' he replied.

'You don't have to downplay your marriage,' she told him. 'I'm not jealous. I'm only glad that you were happy, and if I can make you half as happy in the future, I'll feel fulfilled.'

He had to break away from their embrace when Charlotte came in to say that she had served supper.

'I'm afraid that what you're getting tonight is what's left in the deep freeze,' she told them as she ladled out the stew. 'This is venison that was shot across on Mull,' she informed Rebecca as she passed her the plate. 'You remember how well we feasted here in the summers on gifts of fish and lobsters, Alan,' she reminded him as she served him. 'Are you going to retire?'

Charlotte always had a habit of slipping in questions, as if she wanted to throw people off balance, a technique from her profession as a court lawyer.

'No. I feel I've still got a few years of teaching left in me, and I've still got my book on Hellenistic sculpture to finish.'

'Goodness, is it still not done? I remember you working on it here years ago.'

'I'm making good progress at last,' he assured her.

'And you, Rebecca: what are you going to do with your life when you graduate?'

'I'd like to go into teaching.'

'You're not considering becoming a minister, since you're also studying theology?'

I don't think they would have me, since I'm a Catholic.'

It was as if the fire had gone out suddenly in the room, and the temperature plunged. As they ate in silence he knew that Rebecca had surrendered a major hostage to fortune in that fiercely Protestant family, in which there had been prayers with every meal.

'I hope you get a good price for the house,' he said.

'We'll see. The market's depressed, but it could stay that way for some years, and we need the money, as I told you. On the other hand, Iona's a very popular place. People buy houses here so that they can be buried on the island – among the Scottish kings, they believe. At least we've all had very happy times here. Is there anything you would like from the house as a memento, Alan?'

'I don't think so.'

'There is one thing,' Charlotte said, and left the table. She returned with a framed foot square of stained glass, showing the house from the beach. He remembered the summer that Vivien had worked on it, cutting the glass in her father's workshop, oars resting in the rafters above.

He knew it wasn't being given to him out of generosity. Nor was it a gift for himself alone. It was also to remind Rebecca that he had been happily married to an artistic woman for over thirty years.

'It's beautiful,' his lover enthused as she held it up to the light.

He saw a hallowed summer brought back in the blue of the sea, the flower-carpeted machair around the house.

'I'll wrap it up well for you before you go,' his sister-in-law told him as the coffee percolated with a whispering sound at her back.

Chapter 11

On the day after their visit to Mackilligin's sister-in-law he and his lover went walking round Iona. He wanted to show her the island, and in particular the bay at which St Columba was reputed to have landed to begin his mission in Scotland. It was a blustery morning when they set out from the hotel, waves running swift and high in the sound. They crossed the narrow island to the western machair where members of the monastic community had tended their flocks, wearing hooded surcoats against the weather. The bay is called *Camus cuil an t'Saimh*, the Bay at the Back of the Ocean, and on a summer morning Vivien and he had often swam there naked. But that day rain came sweeping in from the cold Atlantic, and they were sodden as they trekked up and over the hillside to stand above stony Columba's Bay.

They were going to have stayed three days on Iona, but because of his sister-in-law's presence they left the morning after their pilgrimage to the Saint's landing place. Mackilligin was angry with Charlotte for having spoiled their holiday, but he didn't want to give her any more opportunity to spread stories about her widower brother-in-law and his student lover. On the drive back to St Andrews Rebecca complained of not feeling well. He urged her to stay with him, but she insisted that all she required was rest.

The following morning he waited for a call from her, and when he hadn't heard from her by noon, assumed that she was having a long lie-in. He took his mobile to his office, but couldn't concentrate on the lecture he was writing. When she hadn't contacted him by the early evening he was seriously worried. He considered going round to McIntosh Hall to find out if she were all right, but that looked too blatant, so he decided to phone. The warden, whom he knew, answered.

'I'm afraid she's not well.'

'Not well?'

'Who's speaking please?'

'I'm a friend of hers. What's wrong with her?'

'She's running a very high temperature. We've sent for her mother.'

'Thank you,' he said, and put the phone down. He blamed himself for her condition, which must be serious if they felt that they had to send for her mother. But he couldn't have risked asking the warden any more questions. He didn't sleep that night, and he didn't drink much as he sat up in his dressing-gown, wondering how he was going to get more information on his lover's condition without raising suspicion.

He received a text message of two words. *Going home.* No expression of love, no details about how she was. He texted back: *What's wrong, darling?* He left his phone lying on the table in the kitchen, watching it constantly as if his mind could activate it, but it lay there silent. At nine the main phone rang.

'Professor Mackilligin? This is Felicity Campbell-Arthurson, Rebecca's mother. Since you've been so kind to her I thought I should let you know that we've taken Rebecca home from St Andrews because she has pneumonia.'

'Pneumonia?'

'We can't understand how she caught it. She says she's been taking the supplements I bought for her, and as you know the weather in St Andrews has been dry and mild these last few days.'

'She must have caught a chill,' he answered, knowing that he couldn't stay silent.

'I assume so. Anyway, she's home now, and she won't be coming back to St Andrews until she's fully recovered, even if it's after term resumes and she misses lectures. Her health is more important than her degree, and her father can always help her to catch up.'

'Tell her I was asking for her,' he requested.

'I certainly will. She's very fond of you. She was rambling last night and was talking about you. She kept referring to Iona. Were you giving a lecture on Iona?'

Was this a trap? Had Rebecca disclosed their relationship in her delirium?

'Yes I was. I was talking about John Duncan, who did several paintings of Iona.'

'That must be it. Well, I'd better go and see to the invalid. It's been nice speaking with you again. You know, we regard you as being like an uncle to Rebecca. I'll let you know when she's going back to St Andrews.'

He hit the bottle hard that night, not only because he was worried about Rebecca being ill, but also because he wondered what else she had given away in her fever. Suppose she disclosed more before she recovered? Her parents might come to find out that he had taken her to Iona, where she had been soaked to the skin on their pilgrimage to Columba's Bay. As he drank whisky he kept the mobile phone in front of him, in case she was lucid enough to send him a message of reassurance, but when he woke up on the sofa in the cold dawn there was no text.

It could be several weeks into the Candlemas semester before she would be allowed back to St Andrews, and he felt that he couldn't survive that length of time without her. He decided to wait for a couple of days, then phone her mother and find out how she was. In the interim he stayed away from the whisky bottle and concentrated on writing his book.

He called three nights later, to be told that Rebecca was 'improving.' He knew he was taking a chance when he told her mother that he was planning to be in Edinburgh the following weekend to do research, and would like to visit his student.

'I'm sure Rebecca will be very pleased to see you. What time would you like to come?'

At three on the Saturday he was travelling to the Campbell-Arthurson house in a taxi, nervously adjusting his clothing as if he were going to ask for their daughter's hand.

'She's still in bed,' her mother informed him as she led him upstairs. Rebecca was sitting up in bed reading, and when he came in she turned the book upside down on the cover and offered her cheek to be kissed, though he wanted to put his arms round her.

'You gave us a fright,' he told her.

'It started as a heavy cold, then turned into pneumonia.'

'We still don't know how she caught it,' her mother said. 'Thank goodness, she's over the worst now. She keeps fretting about getting back to St Andrews, but the doctor says to give it another week. You're going to have to look after yourself better,' she addressed her daughter.

'What do you mean?' Rebecca demanded.

'I don't think you've been taking the supplements I left with you in the Hall.'

'Sometimes you forget.'

'You can't afford to forget. There are too many infections going around, especially in a hall of residence, where – shall we say? – some of the residents don't look as if they practise very high standards of hygiene. And there are students coming from abroad who bring diseases.'

'In which case I would be better in a flat.'

'We couldn't allow that,' Felicity said firmly. 'At least in the Hall you're supervised to some extent, and if anything goes wrong, there's a warden to call on. What would have happened if you had taken ill in a flat?'

'I could share.'

'You don't have any friends from school at St Andrews, so you don't know the kind of person you could get as a flatmate. They could hold parties, or even be on drugs. And they could be the kind of person who leaves a bathroom in a disgusting state. The Hall is the best option. What do you think, professor?'

It seemed up to that point that they had forgotten he was in the room.

'I agree with you,' he told her, but tried to signal with his eyes to Rebecca that he was only saying this to placate her mother.

'As for your studies, when you come home at weekends your father will help you to catch up in classics. Father O'Brien will help you with your theology studies.'

'My studies are inter-denominational, mother.'

'Father O'Brien is a very clever man who studied in Rome. He's our parish priest,' she explained to their visitor in an aside. 'Would you do something for me, please, professor? I need to go to the chemist to get some more supplements for Rebecca. Could you stay with her until I get back? I won't be longer than twenty minutes.'

'Of course.'

They listened in silence until they heard the front door close, then the car driving away. He lay down on the bed beside her and put his arms round her.

'I've been so worried about you, blaming myself for keeping you out in the bad weather on Iona.'

'I didn't want the warden to phone my parents because I knew my mother would make a big fuss. If they'd let me stay quietly in bed for two days in Hall I would have been fine.'

'But you have pneumonia,' he reminded her.

'Mild pneumonia that can be cleared up in a week or so with antibiotics, instead of these useless supplements she insists on me taking. What she really wanted was to get me home, to dominate me, treating me like a child again. I'm hardly allowed to get out of bed to go for a pee.'

He lay with his arms round her warm inviting body, then lifted back the bedclothes to raise her nightdress and kiss her breasts. In a few minutes he had shed his clothes and was inside her.

'I can't begin to tell you how much I've missed you and how I've worried about you,' he told her as he stroked her hair.

'You'd better put your clothes back on before she comes,' she cautioned him.

'Do your parents like me?' he asked as he pulled on his trousers.

'As far as they're concerned you're a kindly professor who takes an interest in their daughter's studies and welfare. They would never dream that you have designs on me. God, I want to get out of this place and back to St Andrews as soon as possible. I wish I could come with you today.'

'Your mother said another week or so.'

'Yes, but she's liable to turn up unannounced in St Andrews to make sure I'm taking my supplements, which means that we're going to have to be very careful.'

When Felicity came upstairs he was sitting by the bed, giving her daughter a résumé of his lectures which she had missed.

'It's really so kind of you to take such an interest in Rebecca,' she told him as she twisted the safety cap on the container of pills and spilled one out on to her palm, holding it out to her daughter with a glass of water.

'Not at all. I look forward to seeing her back soon in St Andrews.'

On the train home he reflected on his relationship with his lover. There were too many practical problems – their age difference, the excessive control exercised by her mother. He began to wonder if he shouldn't bring the relationship to an end, for Rebecca's sake. It was getting too dangerous, the way in which her parents had made him an honorary member of their family, their daughter's guardian at St Andrews, a trust he had violated. On his visit he hadn't seen any sign that Felicity Campbell-Arthurson was suspicious about his motives in taking such an interest in her daughter, otherwise why would she have left him alone with her in the bedroom? But he had betrayed her by having intercourse with her daughter in the family home.

He sensed that he was in a precarious position, and that he was probably going to have to sacrifice their love for the sake of safety. Yet he knew that Rebecca wouldn't allow him to walk away as if it had been like a fling between two students. He had transformed her, made her sexually active, and had allowed her to articulate her contempt for her parents. She was a much stronger person than the meek student who had knocked his door that first night he had invited her round for a meal.

But in the following week, as he tried to immerse himself in his work to compensate for Rebecca's absence, he knew that he wasn't going to be able to give her up. He had to acknowledge that it wasn't only the emotional bond between them: there was also the satisfaction – and the pride – in going to bed with a young woman, as if in some way he was defeating the ageing process through sex.

She phoned him that night from her bed, using her mobile.

'Can you hear me?'

'Just,' he told her.

'I've made the bedclothes into a tent so that my mother can't hear. Your visit at the weekend has made me feel much better – especially when you came in beside me and gave me a tonic. I'm tired of all these supplements and would like to flush them down the loo, but there would be a hell of a row when she found out that they'd gone. I've got to play it carefully so that I can get back to St Andrews as soon as possible with the minimum of fuss and without supervision. God, I'm feeling so randy, I wish I was in your bed. You will keep it warm for me?'

'Constantly.'

'I hear a heavy tread on the stairs. It's the rugby referee coming to check up on me and to find out if I'm strong enough for a classics lesson. Have to go. Love you to bits.'

The reassuring call gave him the energy and impetus to get on with his academic work. Instead of sitting in the house, brooding on his loneliness, he went back to his office after supper to work until late, the window buffeted by wind, his mobile beside the keyboard in expectation of a call from Edinburgh. But it was ten days before he heard from Rebecca.

'I'm phoning from the Hall. My mother has just gone, having left a bagful of vitamins with the warden, with instructions to see that I take them before meals. If I get my hands on them they're going in the bin.'

'How do you feel?' he asked.

'A little bruised by my involvement in the Punic Wars with my father, but otherwise wonderful.'

'Are you coming round tonight?'

'No, the warden's about and my mother told him to watch that I don't go out in the cold and have a relapse, so I'd better stay in. But I'll be in your lecture in the morning.'

He projected an image of the Esquiline Venus, explaining that it was found in 1874 on the Esquiline Hill in Rome, 'in what was probably part of the site of the Horti Lamiani, one of the imperial gardens, where other classical sculptures have been uncovered. It's believed to be a Roman copy of a Greek original marble statue of Aphrodite. As you can see, the arms are missing. But what position were they in? Well, the remains of the little finger of her left hand are visible on the back of her head. So is this the goddess as bather, tying up her hair in place with her left hand, her right one reaching for the fabric draped over the vessel on her right hand side? The cobra coiled round the vase at her feet reinforces the association with the Greek goddess Aphrodite.

'This statue combines elements of previous schools of sculpture, and particularly the Praxitelean concept of the nude female form. The features, the strong torso, the small high breasts and the thighs pressed together suggest that the statue was inspired by early Hellenistic models. However, I feel that this falls short of the perfect symmetry of a classic Hellenistic Aphrodite sculpture. The body is certainly voluptuous, but the head has what has been called an "archaic severity."' Lord Clark the distinguished art historian said of her: "Her elegant sisters from the metropolis would smile at her thick ankles and thicker waist." He goes on: "the sculptor has discovered what we may call the plastic essentials of the female body.'"

Rebecca stayed behind after the lecture, and told Mackilligin: 'That was a very sexy lecture.'

'Sexy?' he queried.

'Yes. I didn't find your lectures sexy in the beginning, but now I do. Take me to bed.'

Chapter 12

Rebecca began to study stained glasswork under Jessica Rae, sitting beside the artist at the table overlooking the harbour. But there was a problem in this arrangement for Mackilligin: she told him that she wouldn't have the time both to attend his lectures and to learn the craft of stained glasswork. He was dismayed, because he found that she inspired him as she sat smiling at him in the front row of the lecture room. However, he would gain more of her company because she wanted to use Vivien's studio in the house. He would have given her a front door key for access if he weren't there, but was frightened the neighbours would see her using it.

Initially she didn't try her hand at cutting out designs, but sat in the studio reading Vivien's books of instruction. He worked below, hunched over his laptop as he forged ahead with his book, now delayed by more years than he cared to calculate, with the publisher becoming impatient with his excuses. He found it conducive to his creativity to have his lover studying upstairs, and when they wanted a break, they went to bed, or she came downstairs to make coffee. He was pleased that she was beginning to treat his place as her own home, standing in the kitchen at the percolator in her seductive denims and bringing him across the steaming mug.

'Are you making progress at your glass studies?' he enquired as they sat together on the sofa.

'I love it. Jessica explains everything so well. Glass is so beautiful to work with and when you're cutting it you don't feel that you're damaging it. I love the way it changes the light. But I wish she'd let me pay.'

'Jessica has a good heart and wants to encourage the young,' he responded, and left it at that, having come to a private financial arrangement with the stained glass artist with regard to his lover's tuition fees.

He liked the way his life had settled into a pleasant ritual again, as in the years of his marriage. He rose at six, listening to classical music on Radio 3 instead of the Today programme with its car bombs and evasive politicians, where the beauty and depth of the English language were reduced to sound-bites, where correspondents masqueraded as experts in fields from foreign affairs to medicine. It was more therapeutic to shave to Brahms than to listen to the aggressive interviews of John Humphrys.

At eight thirty he slipped his laptop into its black case and headed for his office. He gave a lecture most mornings, and conducted tutorials on two afternoons a week. Lunch was usually a healthy snack from the chilled shelves of Boots, eaten at his desk. On free afternoons he booted up his laptop and worked at his book, when he wasn't listening to students who had problems appreciating statuary. At six he went home and began to prepare supper for himself and his lover, if she were coming round to use the studio.

Some evenings he took up a mug of coffee to the studio, stopping on the threshold because he was struck by the uncanny resemblance between his lover's profile and that of his late wife as she cut out pieces of glass rejects which

Jessica Rae had given to her as exercises. He noticed that Rebecca was unusually subdued, especially in bed.

'Are you worried about something?' he enquired gently.

'No, I'm fine,' she responded in a quiet voice.

'Is your work – I mean, your studies – proving difficult?'

'No, I can keep up, and the lectures are interesting.'

'Are your parents hassling you?'

'I'm fine, darling,' she told him in a tone asking him to desist from questioning her.

He put it down to her slow recovery after the debilitating pneumonia. She had her studies, the demanding continuous assessment courses; her shifts in the coffee shop; the choir; playing the organ; himself; and she was trying to master working with stained glass. But he daren't suggest that she was doing too much.

'We'll have a break in Edinburgh on Saturday,' he told her.

'Why?'

'Because I've been asked to authenticate a marble statue.'

'I can't. I'm working in the coffee shop all day Saturday.'

'Can't you change with someone else?' he asked, irritated.

'No, I've committed myself.'

'What about the following Saturday?'

'All right. Where about in Edinburgh are you going?'

'To a house in Moray Place.'

'So long as we don't run into my parents.'

They went down by train together. The man who opened the door for them in the Moray Place residence explained that one of his ancestors had gone on a Grand Tour in the early nineteenth century, and had purchased the marble statue which stood at the foot of the imposing staircase. The female was covering her right breast with her left hand, her right hand trailing a garment.

'We're moving to a small house and we won't have room for Aphrodite, so we're going to sell her.'

'You know it's Aphrodite?' Mackilligin queried.

'Oh yes, professor. That's what we've always called her. She's like a member of our family. My father used to talk to her when he came in from the Court of Session. I have the original receipt for the purchase in my desk upstairs. It cost fifty pounds, a considerable sum in these days, so I assume that it must be very old.'

'It's a very good copy.'

'A copy?'

Mackilligin was pleased about being able to demonstrate his expertise in front of his lover.

'A copy of Aphrodite of Menophantos, a Roman marble statue of Venus found at a Camaldolese monastery in Rome. The original carries the signature of Menophantos, a Greek sculptor, apparently of the first century BC. That's all that's known about him. Someone made a copy – a good copy – of the original and sold it to your ancestor as an original. Fifty pounds was probably a bargain.'

'What would I get for it at auction?' the owner wanted to know.

The art historian ran his hand up and down the marble buttocks, feeling rough scars left by the chisel.

'I'd say it was executed in the late eighteenth, early nineteenth century. I doubt if an art gallery would buy it, but you might get a couple of thousand from a private collector.'

They left the disappointed owner and went down into the Botanic Gardens.

'You're very quiet today,' Mackilligin observed. 'Is something wrong?'

'My period is twenty days late.'

Her declaration seemed to be amplified through the Gardens, though she spoke in a whisper. His first reaction was to take her in his arms and dance her round.

'Are you sure?'

'Quite sure. You only need simple arithmetic to work it out.'

'*Darling,*' he said ecstatically, hugging her.

'Why do you say that?' she challenged him.

'Because I'm going to be a father at an age when most men - '

'What about me? How am I going to explain it to my parents?'

'We'll find a way,' he reassured her.

'There is no way. They'll be horrified.'

'We need to be certain about this,' he said excitedly. 'We're going to buy a pregnancy kit.'

They went out to find the nearest chemist. He accepted the bland white bag with trembling hands from the assistant behind the counter, and waited outside the child-changing cubicle. Rebecca sat on the toilet with the kit on the baby shelf. She already knew the result, but went through the ritual of the instructions, then waited for the test to develop, her face in her hands. How had this happened? She hadn't wanted to go on the pill, so had relied on her lover to provide protection. The condom must have come off.

'It's positive,' she told him when she came out.

But when he hugged her again she broke away. He was too preoccupied with the idea of fatherhood to understand that she didn't want the baby, because it would mean the end of her studies, since her mother certainly wouldn't look after it. Had he done it on purpose because he wanted to be a father?

They went for lunch at a vegetarian restaurant with a high reputation, but Rebecca would only take a starter.

'I'm frightened, Alan.'

'It'll be all right.' Flushed with wine and fatherhood, he leaned across to pat her hand. 'There are very few complications in childbirth nowadays. I was delivered at home, but you'll be in hospital, with every possible back-up.'

'I don't mean that.'

He abandoned the appetizing risotto.

'You mean an abortion?'

She shook her head. 'I could never do that. My parents are going to go crazy.'

'They'll have to accept it, Rebecca. It's your body, and they have no right to impose decisions about it on you. Whatever needs to be done for you and the baby, I'll do it. And I'm sure that your parents will come round, once they see their grandchild.'

'You don't know my parents,' she said vehemently.

'Then don't tell them just now.'

'They'll have to be told, sooner or later. Remember, they're paying for me at St Andrews.'

'I can do that, darling. If they're going to make that much trouble, forget about them.'

'My father's a fanatical sportsman, the type who never gives up on anything. You haven't seen him in action on the squash court. The way he smashes the ball, you'd think he was trying to kill his opponent with it.'

'They can't harm you. The main thing from now on for us is to concentrate on the baby and to plan for it. It's been an exciting day; let's go home to St Andrews. That's your home – our home – from now on.'

But she was silent on the train, staring unfocused out of the window. Why had she become involved with this man? Because he had seduced her? He had invited her round to his house on the pretext of talking about classical sculpture, and he had her clothes off and into bed that first evening. But she knew that she was as much to blame. She had wanted to experience sex and once she had enjoyed orgasms, she couldn't get enough of them.

'You can stay with me from now on,' he invited her as they alighted from the train.

'I appreciate your offer, but I'll keep my room on in the Hall. I need to think about when I'm going to break the news to my parents.'

'I'll come with you.'

She stopped on the bridge above the line to stare at him in the harsh lighting. She could see the scene: the gentility of afternoon tea in the Morningside villa ended by his announcement that he had made their daughter pregnant and was going to marry her, a man older than her father. Was her lover becoming senile? Did he really believe that the rugby referee would sit smiling and nodding his assent in the special chair from which he watched sport on satellite television? There would be broken cups – and maybe more.

'No, Alan, this is my responsibility.'

By the following Tuesday he had found an architect through Yellow Pages and was showing him round the house, asking his advice about making it infant-friendly.

'The stairs are quite steep,' the architect cautioned. 'You'll need a gate across.'

'What about converting this bedroom into a nursery?'

The architect surveyed it from the doorway.

'If you're going to put your grandchild in here, it needs brightening up.'

The client didn't correct him about the paternity of the occupant.

'I'd put in a Velux window in the roof – if we can get planning permission,' the architect continued. 'The planners are very protective of old properties like this one in St Andrews.'

'How long would planning take to get?' he asked anxiously.

'About three months for the plans to be approved, and then we have to apply for a building warrant. When is the baby due?'

'September.'

'It could be tight, but we can probably get it done by

then. I'll draw up a plan and ask several builders to submit estimates. What about this room?'

The door was open, and the architect saw the stained glass fragments on the table.

'That's my wife's work-room,' Mackilligin explained. 'I don't think she'd want anything done to it.'

The architect was puzzled about the structure of this family, but it wasn't his place to ask such questions.

Mackilligin found that his coming status of fatherhood was an inspiration in delivering his lectures. Suddenly the age gulf between the students sitting listening to him didn't seem so vast. It was gratifying to know that he shared their potency. The news sent him back to his laptop, to resume work on his book on Hellenistic sculpture, his fingers on the keyboard having difficulty keeping up with the flow of ideas. It was as if he were seeing things more clearly, more deeply – as if at last he was beginning to understand life. Men who ordered Viagra from overseas websites must feel the same, he reckoned.

But there was a downside to his new status. When Rebecca came round she wasn't so interested in going to bed with him. She told him that she was feeling tired, though she was still only in the earliest stages of her pregnancy. He was disappointed that he couldn't lead her by the hand upstairs. Instead she went up by herself and sat in Vivien's studio. She wasn't reading any more books on stained glass design, but was doing the more complicated exercises involving small designs which Jessica Rae had set for her, telling Mackilligin, when he met her on Market

Street, that 'your young friend has a natural gift to work in the medium.'

'I'm so pleased to hear that, Jessica.'

'Oh yes, at my exalted age it's very gratifying to come across a young person who'll continue a very old artistic tradition. God willing, Rebecca will do some very fine work in due course.'

When they were having the supper he had cooked they discussed the future.

'I need to tell my parents soon, to get it over with. Once I start putting on weight my mother will notice.'

'That won't happen for a few months.'

'It doesn't matter, I need to do it now.'

'What will their reaction be?'

'They'll dance with joy round the house. For God's sake, Alan, what do you think they'll say? My father sent me here to get a first class degree in classics, and my mother told me when I was at home with pneumonia that she hoped that after taking my degree I would consider becoming a nun because she believed that her prayers and not the antibiotics the doctor insisted I had to have instead of supplements saved me when I had pneumonia. I'm planning to go to tell them next Saturday.'

'I'll come with you to Edinburgh and wait until you've told them.'

'No, Alan, I want to go by myself, to compose myself on the train.' She reached across the table for his hand. 'I'm not rejecting you, and I'm thrilled about the baby, but as you know I have very difficult parents.'

'Whatever happens, I'll stand by you,' he promised.

Chapter 13

All the way to Edinburgh on the train Rebecca was working out her strategy for breaking the news of her pregnancy to her parents. She knew that she had to tell them both together, otherwise her mother would become hysterical, and that would set her father off. Usually she economised by taking a bus, but she allowed herself the luxury of a taxi because she wanted to get the ordeal over with. Instead of putting her own key into the door and surprising them she rang the bell, composing herself on the step.

'You look pale,' her mother remarked as she offered a cheek to be kissed.

'I'm feeling a lot better,' she answered, following her down the hall that seemed alien now with its Catholic imagery of the crucifix and a print of the Last Supper.

Her father was never demonstrative in his welcome. She knew that he would be home today because her mother had told her on the phone that he wasn't required as a referee on the rugby pitch. He didn't switch off the game he was watching, or turn down the volume.

'How are your studies going?' he called to her as he watched a scrum on the flat screen.

'Fine. I've got news for you. I'm pregnant.'

Felicity was setting down the tea tray as the announcement came, and her precious bone china clashed.

'You are *what*?' her father asked, flicking off the remote control.

She repeated herself.

'You'll never be a nun now!' her mother wailed.

'Enough, Felicity,' he warned, holding up a hand as if cautioning a player on the pitch. 'I presume the father's a student.'

'He's a member of the university staff.'

Her mother slumped on the sofa, face in her hands as if attacked by a blinding migraine.

'He seduced you,' the referee said.

'No he didn't.'

This was a man for whom there were no ambiguities or obscurities in a classical text.

'Explain.'

'I told you, he's a member of staff.'

'In classics?' her male parent persisted.

'Oh surely not,' a distraught voice came from the sofa.

'Fel-icity! I told you.' Then, turning to his daughter, who hadn't sat down for the confrontation: 'in which Department?'

She had decided on the journey that she would answer their questions truthfully, since the father's identity would have to come out eventually.

'He's in Art History.'

'Go on,' he ordered, as if telling a pupil to continue with a translation which was taking too much time.

'It's Professor Mackilligin.'

At first Felicity couldn't take in the name, but with the realisation came vocal anguish.

'The fellow who was supposed to be looking after you, who came here and took our hospitality,' the classicist continued. 'He must have seduced you, because an eighteen year old doesn't give herself to a man who must be at least sixty.'

'Sixty one,' she corrected him, as if this were an important detail. She felt strong and confident, now that most of it had come out. 'I love him and we're going to get married.'

Her father shook his head. This was a serious foul, a truly dirty tackle.

'He fed you drink,' the broken voice came from the sofa.

'He did not. He behaved perfectly properly towards me.'

'So you seduced him?' Diarmid Campbell-Arthurson said with a sneer. 'You went along to his house and climbed into his bed.'

'You're cheapening it,' his daughter warned.

'It's you who've cheapened yourself and brought disgrace on this house,' the voice, stronger now, accused from the sofa. 'We brought you up with moral values and sent you to a good school. Is this how you repay us? You are *not* going to have this baby.'

'I will not have an abortion.'

'Who said anything about an abortion? We're devout Catholic people who believe in the sanctity of life, and we will not have an abortion on our consciences. You'll take a year out from your studies, and when your time comes, I'll take you to London to have the child, and it can go for adoption.'

'I am going to keep this baby, mother.'

'You certainly are not. I'm not going to have this family talked about as if you're a tramp.'

'You'll do as your mother says,' he came in.

Their daughter shook her head, feeling that she had the advantage on them, since she was on her feet.

'I'm keeping our child and marrying Alan.'

'You're not marrying a man ten years older than me; you're a minor and don't know your own mind because you've been seduced by that bastard,' the referee delivered his decision.

'He's not a bastard; he's a decent honourable man.'

'This is the man we invited to our house, the man I confided in, the man I left alone in her bedroom with my daughter!' her mother was crying.

'A bloody artist,' her father said contemptuously.

Their daughter looked round the prim room she had come to loathe.

'I'm going. I'm sick of carpets that are covered in polythene, sick of rugby matches roaring from that flat screen on the wall.'

'Walk out and there won't be a penny of support,' her mother warned.

And then she walked out. She didn't go upstairs to her bedroom to collect any of her belongings or say goodbye to the labrador. She was trembling with every step because she was sure he would come after her and haul her back. But when she was safely on the other side of the front door she leaned against the wall and thought: *where did I find the courage to do this*?

That evening in St Andrews her lover listened to her story about the confrontation with apprehension as well as admiration, because he was the cause of her breaking with her parents, and it was now his entire responsibility to look after her. Had she given him this honest account to remind him of this responsibility towards her, and to the child they were expecting?

The following evening, when she came round to his house, she found him at work on his Hellenistic sculpture study.

'I forgot to add, though I expect you deduced it, that my parents are going to cut off my financial support, so I'm going to increase my hours in the coffee shop, and I'll arrange a student loan.'

'I don't want that,' he said firmly. 'You've got to concentrate on having the baby.' He put a palm on her stomach. 'It's wonderful to think that it's growing in here as we speak. Before you start to carry the extra weight I think we should take a holiday in the Easter break.'

'Have you anywhere in mind?'

'It's your choice. Tell me where you want to go and I'll make the arrangements.'

She told him that ever since she was a child, she had been fascinated by stories of St Francis of Assisi. She recalled sitting enthralled in primary school as the teacher told how in a dense ravine near his hermitage in Umbria the Italian saint had had a night-long contest with a nightingale, each trying to outdo the other to the glory of God. Francis was weary and hoarse by the dawn, and had to admit defeat.

'Some afternoons in the university library I go online,' Rebecca revealed. 'A web camera's been set up in the streets of Assisi, and I can see the weather and follow the movements of locals and tourists. In fact, before meeting you I'd decided to ask my parents for a trip to Assisi as a twenty first birthday present, but I knew my mother would insist on coming. She would see such a pilgrimage as a prelude to her daughter entering a convent.'

'Assisi? That sounds very interesting. I'll make a booking for a week in April. We can fly out and stay in a hotel.'

Next morning he went round to the travel agent. They would fly from Edinburgh to Rome and either take the train from the Italian capital, or hire a car there for the two hour drive to Assisi. Mackilligin left the agent to work out the details. They had agreed that they would be married before they went on holiday, and he discussed the requirements of a registry wedding over the phone, fixing up a date in April. But when was he going to tell his colleagues? That was the question on his mind as he sat in his office, not writing on his laptop but musing on his great good fortune in having fallen in love for the second time in his life, and, for the first time, becoming a father. Neither of the two events showed disrespect for his late wife.

He was preparing the supper for two that evening when he heard the knock on the door.

'Wait a minute – ' he protested as Diarmid Campbell-Arthurson pushed past him.

'You seduced my daughter, you bastard.'

'Get out!' Mackilligin ordered the intruder.

The rugby referee twisted the art historian's arm up his back and propelled him into the nearest room, the kitchen.

'You took advantage of my daughter.'

'Rebecca and I are getting married,' Mackilligin told him through the pain in his arm.

'I don't think you'll be fit enough for marriage when I'm finished with you.'

Mackilligin was thrown back against the kitchen unit, his head whiplashing, striking the extractor hood, activating the mournful fan. The bottle of virgin olive oil he had been cooking with spilt on the quarry tiles and as he slipped he was kicked in the testicles. As he went down, holding his privates in agony, he heard what he took to be the bone in his nose going under a fist. He sprawled in his blood mingling with the virgin oil and heard the room being trashed. He saw books swept from his shelves and heard the implosion of his television screen as a brogue went through it. He tried to shout as he saw his laptop raised above his attacker's head, and then it smashed into the wall.

After his assailant had banged the front door behind him Mackilligin lay in the wreckage. He could see blood trickling from the wound at his temple on to the tiles, among the smashed crockery. He turned his head in slow painful motion and saw his laptop, its guts hanging out, and he knew that he had lost three years work on his Hellenistic book, not having made a back-up copy. The silence was eerie, as people report after an earthquake. Yet there was something restful in lying there, slightly concussed from the umpire's fists. He heard feet passing over the cobbles outside the window, but didn't shout for help.

Was he lying in the wreckage of his life, the art historian

pondered? Had it been a terrible mistake to have become involved with a student, and to make her pregnant? He imagined his late wife coming through the door and finding him lying there. She wouldn't have shouted at him, but would have shaken her head and told him that he was an old fool as she helped him up. The synapses in his head were firing with dizzy random, the result of the blow, and his vision was out of focus. Where was his attacker now? Driving back to Edinburgh, or seeking out his daughter to tell her that he had taken revenge for her seduction?

Mackilligin seemed to drift into exhausted sleep, disturbed by the door opening. Was this his assailant back? He turned his head and saw his lover's shapely butt in her denims. She screamed as she rushed towards him.

'Are you drunk?'

'No, perfectly sober,' he told her quietly, with an idiotic smile. 'I had a visit from your father.'

'He did this to you?' she wailed, kneeling beside him, her fingers running through her hair in her distress. Then, decisively, getting up: 'I'm going for the police.'

'No, don't, 'he restrained her with a painful arm.

'He's got to pay for his bullying at last. I've been enduring it for years – not the physical type, but the psychological blows which are just as painful. You can't walk into someone's house and beat them up and wreck the place without paying the price.'

'It'll only make things worse if you bring in the police,' he cautioned her. 'I'll have to explain why he attacked me.'

'But it's my business, how I decide to conduct my life,' she said vehemently.

'Help me up,' he pleaded.

'Are you sure there aren't any bones broken?' she asked as he winced.

He touched his nose, but couldn't be sure.

She half carried him, slithering through the broken crockery and spilt virgin oil to the sofa.

'Your face is a terrible mess,' she told him. 'I really think I should get the police. A brute like that shouldn't get away with this.'

'It'll just make more trouble,' he sighed, and asked her to lift the mirror from the wall.

He saw the cut made by the signet ring under the left eye.

'I don't think it needs a stitch,' he spoke into the mirror.

Rebecca boiled a kettle and filled a bowl. Vivien had always been well organised. She maintained that a stained glass artist had to be, working with pieces like a jigsaw. There was a small red fire extinguisher standing in a corner on the top, and below it, in a cupboard, a first aid box. His lover sat beside him on the sofa as she bathed his face with cotton wool from which she squeezed the blood in swirls into the bowl.

'I think you should show this to your doctor.'

'No,' he said hastily. 'He'll ask me how I got it and then there'll be an inquisition.'

'I'll have to put a plaster over it in case it becomes infected.'

He picked up the mirror again and examined his face,

made even older and more unattractive by its injuries, he thought. The plaster was so large that he would be asked what had happened. There was even blood in the eyebrows he had meant to clip. His face depressed him and he put down the mirror.

'What did he say to you?' Rebecca wanted to know when she had shovelled and mopped up the debris on the floor and made coffee.

'Not very much. He got stuck in right away. Anyway, he's gone, no doubt satisfied with his handiwork.'

'I doubt if he's driving home, Alan.'

'What do you mean?'

'I suppose it's the psychology of the sportsman. You don't ease off until you've thrashed your opponent into the ground. He'll be making trouble with the university authorities.'

'He can't do me any harm.'

'I wouldn't count on that. You need to go to bed.'

'I'll be fine,' he reassured her.

She hadn't noticed his laptop under the chair until she brought it to him in two halves.

'It's the only copy of my book I have.'

'Oh no! Maybe the technical people can save the hard drive, though it looks badly damaged,' she pronounced, the disk hanging by an umbilical cord of cable. 'Why didn't you make a copy?'

'I kept meaning to buy one of these little memory sticks you shove in and save your files on, but I didn't get round to it.'

'How long would it take you to rewrite the book?'

'Nine months?'

'This is criminal damage. You should let me get the police.'

'No,' he repeated, though not out of magnanimity. He didn't want a young constable sitting on his sofa, writing down the answers to his questions. *Why did Mr Campbell-Arthurson assault you? Because I'm a sixty one year old professor who seduced his daughter, who is my student.* Did you provoke him in any way? Do you wish to press charges of assault and criminal damage?

'So what are we going to do now?' Rebecca asked.

'What do you mean?'

'Well, he's beaten you up once, and if you don't complain to the police and finish with me, he could come back.'

'I can take care of myself.'

'Can you?' she asked, picking up the mirror. 'You've got to go about with a face like that – and it could get worse. I don't want to see you getting hurt again.'

'If you leave me it'll hurt far more than the beating I've just had.'

'But if it's for your own good?'

'My own good is to continue with you. I promise you: if your father comes near me again I'll call the police.'

'You may not have time to. Next visit he could kill you. He could have killed you today, if your head had struck the tiles on the floor when you fell.'

'I was cooking when he arrived, and the olive oil bottle broke. The floor was like a skating rink.'

'That's not the point. I was going to say: that brute doesn't know his own strength, but of course he does; he's always known it. He knows exactly the weight on the dumbbells he can push up off his chest in the gym, and he knows exactly the number of kilometres he can run on the treadmill. He knows exactly what he's going to do in his next lesson, and he knew exactly what he was going to do when he drove up to St Andrews today. He's so cunning that next time he would make it look like an accident that couldn't be traced back to him.'

'Can we stop talking about your father?' he asked wearily, his head beginning to throb. 'Let's talk about ourselves. Talk positively. You're going to have a baby; that's what matters. We need to fix a date for the wedding at the registry office, and we need to make arrangements about paying your fees. We've got to get back to normal, darling, to show your parents that we won't be intimidated.'

Chapter 14

Having restored the kitchen and made them omelettes for supper, Rebecca went back to the hall at eight. Mackilligin sat with a whisky, mourning the probable loss of his Hellenistic sculpture book when the knocker sounded. He wondered if his assailant had been hiding in the street and had seen his daughter coming and going.

'Who's there?' he called apprehensively from behind the door.

'Jock Stimson,' was the muffled reply.

Stimson was his line manager, but had never visited him at home before. Mackilligin knew there was trouble as he led his visitor into the lounge and asked if he would take a drink.

'I'll have some whisky, if you have it.'

'Talisker?'

'That would be very appealing.'

The art historian had always liked this shrewd but scrupulously fair man who had been a lecturer in chemistry, but preferred the human variety, and had switched to administration. He was now an indispensable member of the Principal's team.

'What on earth happened to your face?' Stimson enquired as he was brought a substantial malt, with a jug of water.

'I fell down the stairs.'

Mackilligin could see that his caller didn't find this convincing, but nevertheless he nodded.

'Have you had stitches?'

'No, it's not as bad as that under the plaster.'

'You could have damaged your eye,' he remarked. 'I had a visitor today,' he announced as he set down his whisky, having sampled it. 'A Mr Campbell-Arthurson.'

His host nodded sadly, having feared what was coming.

'He made a terrific scene in the secretaries' office, demanding to see the Principal. He wouldn't take their word for it that the Principal was away at a meeting, and they had to show him the empty office. That's when I came on the scene, and I took him into my office. He made a serious accusation against you, Alan.'

'Oh yes?' But it didn't sound at all casual.

'He claimed that you seduced his daughter, who's a student of yours.'

'Correction: she's not formally a student of mine. She sometimes sits in on my lectures.'

'Distinction noted. He claimed that his daughter is pregnant by you.'

'She is.'

Stimson took another sip and set down the glass carefully. He was waiting for more than an acknowledgement, and Mackilligin was shifting uncomfortably in his seat, as though his limbs were hurting after his thrashing.

'It's not what you think. We love each other.'

'I'm not thinking anything,' Stimson informed him. 'I'm trying to get at the facts. Because it looks very bad for you. It's very fortunate that Mr Campbell-Arthurson didn't get to the Principal before I collared him.'

'I appreciate your intervention, Jock.'

'He demanded that you be sacked for having seduced his daughter and said that if we didn't do anything, he would contact members of the Court. I pointed out to him that it wasn't a matter for the Court, and as for the Principal's Office, we would note and investigate his complaint, but really, his daughter was over eighteen and therefore an adult, and for this reason, we couldn't discuss her with him, even though he was her parent.'

'I'm grateful to you for this, Jock,' Mackilligin told him.

'He was furious and started shouting that the university was responsible and that he would go to the newspapers. This is a very tricky situation, Alan, which could attract damaging publicity, not only to the university, but to yourself. Think how the tabloids would portray it.' He stretched out an imaginary headline. 'Prof seduces St Andrews student.'

'I didn't force her into my bed,' Mackilligin protested.

'I'm not saying you did, but it's serious.'

'Have you spoken about this to the Principal?' Mackilligin wanted to know.

'I haven't, because I believe that I won't have to involve the Principal if I can have your co-operation.'

'What do you mean – co-operation?' Mackilligin asked, beginning to distrust this man.

'I think you should retire.'

He was about to deliver an explosive reply, but Stimson held up his hand. He had never once raised his voice from its calm level during their conversation.

'You're sixty one. Quite a number of staff go at sixty. I looked into it before I left the office, but I'm afraid that we can't give you a deal because you're over age, and besides, the days of generous retirement packages have gone, at least as far as this university is concerned. But you'll get your normal pension entitlement.'

'This is a stitch-up,' Mackilligin complained bitterly. 'It makes it look as if I'm a guilty man.'

'It's not a stitch-up: it's a way of making it easier on you – and your student friend. The Principal is a very honourable person and would feel bound to have the matter investigated.'

Mackilligin sat in silence after his visitor had finished. He wasn't angry with Stimson: he knew that the administrator was acting with his best interests at heart, and that he was correct in what he had said about tabloid publicity, which would shock Rebecca and could put the unborn baby at risk. His anger was directed against that bastard Campbell-Arthurson, who hadn't been satisfied with the brutal beating, but had gone straight round to the administrative building to finally shaft his daughter's seducer. Rebecca had been right: there was no end to her father's determination and ruthlessness.

'I appreciate you coming round this evening, Jock,' he said eventually. 'When should I go?'

'How many more lectures are you committed to giving?'

'Two more in my Hellenistic statuary course.'

'Which takes us into March,' the administrator calculated. 'Go at Easter. I'll have a publicity statement put out about your distinguished teaching and research – which is true. You've helped to make Art History a five star School in the ratings. One piece of advice: don't as yet tell your colleagues about your partner being pregnant, otherwise they'll think you're being pushed.'

'Which I am,' he said cynically.

'Not pushed, helped,' Stimson corrected him, and, the tricky business done, attended to his whisky before departing with a hand on Mackilligin's shoulder.

Mackilligin didn't tell his lover that her father had gone to the university's administration and that he had been forced to retire to prevent his exposure for seducing a student. Instead he told her that he had decided to take early retirement, so that they could prepare for the arrival of their child, and also because he needed to begin rewriting his book, since IT Services had told him that they couldn't retrieve the data from his wrecked laptop.

'When are you retiring?' Rebecca asked.

'I'm going to go at Easter. That's more convenient for the university.'

'Will they replace you?'

'That's up to them. We live in an age of cut-backs, so they may try to get by on the number of teaching staff they have already.'

'I phoned home last night.'

'Was that wise?' he asked apprehensively.

'I asked to speak to my father and I told him: you could have killed the man I love, the father of my child. You're very lucky that he isn't pressing charges of assault against you "He deserved it for what he's done to you – and us," he said. Then my mother came on and pleaded: "come home this weekend and we'll try to sort things out," but I told her that I'd never set foot in their house again, and that they were to burn the things in my bedroom. I'm going to ring off, I told her. "So who's going to pay for you at university now?" she asked. That's none of your business, I said. ' "We'll make you a ward of court. You aren't twenty one yet." I'm afraid that I lost my temper at that stage and shouted at her: Don't talk such fucking nonsense! "Where did you learn such language?" she asked. "And you were the little girl that I wanted so much to become a nun." I wasn't allowed to choose my own spiritual path, I told her, and besides, I said, the way you've treated me, you're a sham Catholic, on your knees in the church and taking the Body and Blood of Christ into your mouth while all the time you were controlling another human being – even dictating her prayers. "That's a wicked thing to say, girl." That's when I cut her off. I felt strong as I went up to my room, but I sensed that these two won't give up so easily. My father can be far down in a squash game, but he'll continue to smash the ball with the same fury, as if he's determined to demolish the wall. Either or both could appear in St Andrews, so I'm going to have to be ready for them and their tricks.'

'It perhaps wasn't a good idea to contact them,' he said mildly.

'But he attacked you, Alan. He can't get away with it.'

He needed to change the conversation. 'We'll get away

to Assisi at Easter. I've booked a nice hotel.'

'I don't want to go to a hotel. I'd like to stay in a convent.'

'I didn't know one could stay in a convent,' he said, surprised. 'I thought that nobody got into these places, and the nuns didn't get out.'

'I read in a book that convents in Italy take in guests.'

'OK, let's see,' he said, and went into Google on his new laptop. He keyed in religious accommodation Assisi and found a list which he read out to her as he scrolled down.

'The Sisters of Atonement Retreat House sounds interesting,' Rebecca said. 'Can you find out more information about them?'

He read out that it was run by an American order of nuns.

'I'd like to go there, Alan, because then there won't be a language problem.'

He sent an e-mail to the Atonement retreat house. 'I hope we get a quick reply, so that I can make the travel arrangements,' he told his lover. 'Now, should we change our plans and get married in Assisi?'

He had a reply from Italy that afternoon, as he informed Rebecca when she came round in the evening.

'Someone must be watching over us. The Atonement Sisters tell me that they've been fully booked for Easter since last year, but an hour before my e-mail came in, they had the cancellation of a double room through illness. I accepted instantly.'

The following morning he went round to the travel agent to cancel the hotel reservation and finalise their travel arrangements, then walked to the registrar's office to confirm the date of their wedding, the day before they were due to fly out to Italy. Everything seemed to be going well, he thought as he made his way along North Street to his next appointment, to learn what his annual university pension would be, and the size of his lump sum. It seemed to him to be a lot of money, especially when it was explained to him that if he invested the lump sum wisely, he could take his annual pension to over thirty thousand.

However, he still had to face his colleagues in the art building, the plaster still on his face.

'When I fell down the stairs I decided it was time to retire, so I'm going at Easter,' he made light of it.

'We'll miss you,' one of his female colleagues, a noted authority on Raphael, spoke sincerely for the rest of them sitting round the coffee table. 'Maybe you'll come back in and do some part-time teaching. We need your expertise in classical sculpture.'

'I don't think I'll be able to. When I had this accident on the stairs – I was actually answering the door – I had my laptop under my arm and when I fell it smashed and damaged the hard drive. Though the boffins in computing tried their best, they couldn't salvage the hard drive.'

'No back up?' a professorial colleague asked in surprise.

'I kept meaning to, but thought everything would be safe on a modern laptop. I was even offered storage facilities on the BT server on a special secure vault, but I didn't take them up on it. So I'm going to have to begin the book again as soon as I retire, which means going over my notes again and turning them into readable prose.'

'We'll need to have a retirement dinner for you, Alan.'

'I don't want any fuss,' he told them, holding up his hands. 'It's not as if I'll be leaving St Andrews. I'll call in from time to time to hear your news and let you know how my book's progressing.'

He didn't tell them that he was getting married to one of his students who was pregnant by him, because he knew that some of his colleagues – the ones who followed the mace into St Salvator's Chapel on Sundays – would be shocked.

Because her parents would no longer be paying her Hall fees, Rebecca moved in with him. She began to use Vivien's room as a study as well as a studio while he sat downstairs, beginning his book again. Twice a week she walked along to Jessica Rae's house, where she was complimented on how quickly and easily she was learning the art of working with stained glass. Sitting beside the old woman, watching her deft fingers assembling the various coloured pieces into a design was therapeutic for her.

'Alan and I are getting married at Easter,' she disclosed.

'I'm very glad. You'll be very good for each other.'

But she didn't tell her teacher that she was pregnant.

When she returned her lover would be wearing his plastic apron decorated with ducks as he prepared supper, and afterwards, instead of sitting talking with him, she went upstairs to study. He didn't take this as a sign that she was cooling towards him, because he was preoccupied with getting into the creative flow of his book again. Though he was only a few pages into the first chapter, he sensed that it wasn't as insightful as the first version destroyed by the vengeful father.

Rebecca and he were married in the registry office in St Mary's Place on a Friday. He hadn't asked any of his colleagues to be witnesses, and instead two assistants from the building stood in. Even up until the last moment, when they exchanged rings, and in the way she kept looking at the door, he feared that Rebecca expected her father to come crashing through to launch another assault on his daughter's seducer, to stop him becoming her husband. The following morning they flew out for their Assisi honeymoon. There was no delay to the flight, and they picked up the hired car at Rome Airport. Rebecca did the navigation on the two hours' drive, the continental atlas open on her lap. He was a forceful driver, and several times his lover closed her eyes, waiting for the collision.

'Don't forget you're driving on the other side of the road,' she cautioned him.

Neither of them would forget the sight of Assisi spread over the hill as they approached it across the Umbrian plain. The retreat house of the Sisters of Atonement had a security system for its tall gates, and one of the nuns came out to meet them. Rebecca was surprised and pleased that the young woman wasn't wearing black, but a blouse and skirt, and she didn't seem taken aback by the discrepancy in age of the new arrivals.

'This is a beautiful building,' Mackilligin enthused as they were led up to their room.

'If you'd seen it after the earthquake, you would have

despaired. The floors literally opened under our shoes, and we've had years of fund-raising to restore it.'

He was disappointed to see that the room contained single beds, but he made no request for another room. Rebecca opened the doors and went out on to the balcony, to look down on the Basilica of Santa Chiara, with a haze on the plain beyond.

'This is enchanting.'

As they were unpacking the bells of the basilica below began to ring. He put his hands over his ears at the deafening proximity, but his new wife stood on the balcony, her arms raised in exultation. She adored Assisi. Their day began with coffee and new bread in the vaulted dining-room below, the nuns chatting as they served, ordinary woman in touch with and devoted to the flawed world.

'You must love living here,' Rebecca said wistfully to Sister Constance, the youngest, who hailed from Kentucky.

'We love meeting people and making them happy. And the town people are so friendly. I'm learning Italian and they're so patient with me.'

The couple wandered the town in the mild weather, sitting at tables in the squares, having coffee and pastries. He had never felt so relaxed, perhaps because he saw how much his wife was enjoying the experience. On Holy Thursday evening they went up to the Last Supper liturgy at the Cathedral of San Rufino. At the end of the Mass two of the priests climbed up the scaffolding and lifted the figure of Christ from the cross. Mackilligin watched in wonder as the Saviour's arms were freed and folded over His chest as

He was laid upon a canopied bier, looking life-like with His sorrowful expression and crown of thorns. Local women approached the bier, laying flowers at his feet, and men knelt to kiss His hand.

'We must follow the *Processione del Cristo Morto* tomorrow morning,' he whispered to his wife.

Early the following Good Friday morning they ascended to the Cathedral of San Rufino again. The bier containing Christ was hoisted upon the shoulders of bearers who carried His figure through the streets of Assisi, stopping at the Basilica of Santa Chiara where the cloistered Poor Clare nuns opened their doors so that they could pay homage to their faithful Spouse to whom they had devoted their lives. The bier was then carried through the city of Assisi, stopping at several other cloistered convents along the way. Its final destination was the Basilica of Saint Francis. The statue of Christ rested there throughout the day for adoration, until later that same evening when the statute of His mother, the Madonna Addolorata, swords piecing her heart, was carried down through the dark streets of Assisi by torchlight to be with her Son at the Basilica of Saint Francis. Hooded men were carrying penitent crosses, the Confraternities in colourful cloaks accompanying the Madonna. A solemn drum was beaten as the procession, lit by flaming torches, moved slowly through the narrow medieval streets, little candle-lights left flickering on window sills. The Madonna and her Son were united in the Basilica of St Francis, and on that same night, in pitch-darkness with only torches lighting the way, the Bishop of Assisi led both the bier and the statue of the Madonna back to the Cathedral of San Rufino, escorted by the crowds of Assisians and visitors.

'It was a bit overdone,' Mackilligin told his wife.

'What do you mean – overdone?' Rebecca rounded on him. 'It's the most moving thing I've ever experienced in my life.'

While Mackilligin rested on the bed in the warm afternoon, his sleep disturbed by the bells of Santa Chiara, Rebecca visited other churches, and in the early evening the St Andrews chorister went to sit in the side chapel of Santa Chiara to hear the Poor Clares singing Vespers. When she came back she sat on his bed and explained how she couldn't see the nuns because the grille was to the side, enthusing about the beauty of their voices and how mysterious, how withdrawn from the world and how pure they were.

'You almost make it sound as if you would have liked to have been a nun,' her husband remarked.

Chapter 15

Mackilligin regretted coming to Assisi because of the effect it was having on his wife. When he approached her bed for sex she made the excuse that she was tired. He heard her sighs and began to worry that she was lying in the Umbrian darkness, full of doubts and regrets about the course her life was taking. She had always resisted her mother's determination that she was to become a nun, because the ones she had met through the church seemed narrow in their outlook, but the Sisters of Atonement were different, friendly and concerned. They told Rebecca how they were out and about in America, where the mother convent was, helping the poor and needy.

As she lay in bed beside the balcony in the Assisi retreat house, the shutters open so that the bells of Santa Chiara below would waken her, Rebecca could see herself on the street on a summer afternoon, in cool garments, her head covered, a basket over her arm as she shopped for food for the retreat house guests, greeting the locals in Italian.

'I'd love to live here,' she told her husband wistfully as they ate supper in a restaurant housed in an old arched building where wool from the Umbrian plain had been stored in centuries past.

'What would you do about your studies at St Andrews?'

She shrugged. 'Transfer to the university in Perugia. It's not far from here.'

'But you don't speak Italian.'

'I could learn.'

Mackilligin didn't pursue the topic. This climate was too hot for him, even at Easter. The nuns who were his hostesses had told the couple from St Andrews that in the summer Assisi could be a furnace, its narrow streets trapping a ferocious heat that turned an ice in its dish to mush within minutes. He had never been comfortable with heat, and during exceptionally warm summers on Iona with his late wife, when the white sands threatened to blind him, he had remained indoors reading. How could they bring up a baby in such a climate? He couldn't see himself in a straw hat, pushing a buggy with a querulous infant past shops whose walls were covered with crucifixes and tiles depicting St Francis with birds on his raised arms. The place had charm, certainly, but only for a holiday.

'Would you like to live here?' Rebecca prompted as she finished her *zabaglione*.

'I'd miss St Andrews,' he confessed. 'It's a town that grows on you. Don't you feel the same?'

'I like St Andrews, but I'm not sure I'd like to spend the rest of my life there.'

It was the voice of the young, the adventurous, speaking. St Andrews was a town for the elderly, the retired, a place to trundle a bag of golf clubs over the world-famous Old Course. Young people nowadays thought nothing of hitching half-way round the world, of sleeping rough, of eating the simplest fare. It was a thought that made Mackilligin feel old as he sat eating dessert in the vaulted restaurant in Assisi. The woman opposite him, licking the spoon after her *zabaglione*, could be his grandchild. The downside of coming to spiritual places like Rome and Assisi was that one became conscious of one's mortality.

On the last day of their holiday they climbed the steep road up Monte Subasio to the Carceri. Rebecca explained that the hermitage was St Francis's place of retreat, where he could commune with the birds. The incline was making her husband feel his age, and he suggested stopping at the wayside café on the pretext of having a coffee. When the Carceri came in sight round the bend Rebecca crossed herself, to his irritation. In the small chapel a Mass for German pilgrims was in progress, but Rebecca entered in time to receive the Host. He wanted to descend to the town again, but she took the stony path beside the hermitage, into the wood, where, she informed him, Francis's disciples had slept in holes in the ground.

'I wonder where the tree was that the birds gathered on to hear the saint preach,' she speculated.

'You don't believe that.'

'Why not?' She stopped to confront him. 'Birds are part of God's creation. Why shouldn't people be able to communicate with them? Just listen,' she enthused, raising her face. 'The trees are throbbing with their song.' She spent an hour photographing the hermitage and the woods with her digital camera while he rested on a bench, becoming more and more impatient.

'Will we go back down now?' he called to her.

'I haven't finished,' she replied, steadying in the small window of the camera the cross that had been set up in the wood. 'I could stay here for the rest of my life.'

'You would miss Scotland.'

'What would I miss about it?' she challenged him as she reviewed the image she had just taken.

'You would miss St Andrews.'

'You mean the atmosphere? This place is much more spiritual than St Andrews. The Apostle didn't live or die in St Andrews; only his relics were brought there. But St Francis was here. You can sense his presence – almost as if you expect him to walk out from among the trees with birds singing on his shoulders.'

'What about your friends?' he asked.

'The few friends I have at the university, you mean? They aren't interested in spiritual things. All they want to do is to have a good time at university and get a well paid job in the City after they graduate.'

'One has to live in the real world,' he pointed out.

'That depends on what you take to be real,' she argued, coming to sit beside him. 'This remote place is much more real to me than the streets of St Andrews with their shops and cafés. You should become a Catholic.'

The proposition took him by surprise.

'Why?'

'Because it would be good for you.'

'What does that mean?'

'It would give your life a shape, a purpose.'

'But I have that already, with you – and the baby,' he told her, reaching across to touch her stomach.

'I mean a spiritual purpose.'

'So I'm not spiritual enough for you? What do you want

me to do? Go to the barber's, get a tonsure and wear a blanket and sandals in the streets of St Andrews?'

'You know I don't mean that. You live too much in the world of art.'

'That's where my interests lie – where they've always lain. You sound as if you're wanting me to change to an ideal that you have. I can't be that person, Rebecca.'

But she had moved away to take a photograph of the ilex wood in the ravine below the hermitage. They were silent as they tramped back down the hill in the sapping heat. He felt the tension between them, as if a wrong word would cause a major argument. When they were back in Assisi he went to rest and she hurried down to Santa Chiara to catch her last Vespers with the heavenly voiced Sisters. She was saddened at the thought that they were having to leave Assisi, which was changing her in ways which she didn't yet understand.

Back in St Andrews she resumed her studies, and he remained in the house instead of going to his office. But this wasn't the retirement that he had imagined. He had seen himself rising early and going for a long walk along the West Sands before making a healthy breakfast, then opening his laptop to finish his book. He had also expected to continue to receive invitations to speak at conferences at home and abroad on Hellenistic sculpture. One had come from Venice, but he knew he couldn't leave his new wife in her expectant state in case anything went wrong. Instead of having peace and leisure he found himself shopping for both of them, lugging two green hemp bags instead of one from the supermarket and having to prepare the evening meal because she was either studying upstairs in the studio or having a stained glass tutorial with Jessica Rae.

He was also anxious about money. His pension had seemed to him generous and would have given him a comfortable lifestyle as a single person. But out of his income he had to support Rebecca since her parents wouldn't help her. He had committed himself to adapting the house for the baby, having already incurred a bill from the architect. The estimates he received shocked him. The cheapest was for eighteen thousand pounds, and would have to be paid for out of his lump sum, which he had intended to leave untouched, using the interest it earned to augment his pension. He didn't discuss his anxieties with Rebecca because it was his duty to support her, having made her pregnant and having married her.

Rebecca came in one evening with a letter.

'This was sent to me at McIntosh Hall, and one of my friends brought it to me. It's from my mother.'

'More abuse, presumably,' he said, glancing up from his laptop.

'Read it for yourself,' she invited him, tossing it to him.

Dear Rebecca,

I phoned Hall last night, to be told that you had moved out, though your term's rent has been paid in advance. I presume that you are living with the father of your child, a source of great sorrow, shame and disappointment to your father and me. We are still asking ourselves where we went wrong in your upbringing, when matters have turned out so badly. We presumed that we were doing our best by you in guiding you, but evidently not, when you would allow a man over three times your age to part with your precious virginity, thereby destroying any possibility of you becoming a nun, a Bride of Christ. In the trauma of your last visit home I did not have the opportunity to tell you that I visited your seducer in his office in St Andrews, and asked him to look after you, which he assured me he would do, yet all the time he had designs on you and betrayed us.

When he raised his eyes from the letter Rebecca was standing over him.

'You didn't tell me that my mother had paid you a visit.'

'I didn't know how to,' he confessed.

'You mean – you didn't trust my reaction?'

'It's not important, Rebecca.'

'It's very important to me, because it's a matter of trust. I've told you all about my upbringing, and the problems with my parents, yet you withheld this information from me. Weren't you a little ashamed?'

'Ashamed of what?' he asked uneasily, having never seen her in this mood before.

'Ashamed that you were hypocritical, no doubt telling her that, yes, you would look after me and protect me, when you had already been to bed with me.'

'I was trying to protect us both,' he said weakly.

'No, you were trying to protect yourself, Alan.'

He had never had a significant argument with Vivien. But

Rebecca wasn't going to let the subject drop.

'It was a difficult situation, Rebecca.'

'It was a situation that took courage, and you didn't show courage.'

'What should I have done?' he wanted to know.

'What should you have done?' she repeated his plea with surprise. 'You should have refused to see my mother. That would have shown loyalty to me.'

'I didn't have a choice, Rebecca. The secretary told her that I was in, and having come that far, she was obviously prepared to sit and wait until I was free. There was no way out of my office apart from through the secretary's.'

'I don't think you're telling the truth, Alan.'

'What was I expected to do – climb out of my window?' he asked forcibly.

'You know damn well I didn't mean that. You thought she'd got wind of the fact that I was sleeping with you, and that she had come to confront you. You thought your career was on the line.'

'Of course I didn't know what she wanted.'

But that admission wasn't sufficient to stop the relentless interrogation. He was cowed because he hadn't seen this formidable side of Rebecca before, and it occurred to him – though he could never say it to her – that as she stood there, demanding answers, she sounded like the insufferable mother she had described to him, but which was not his recollection of the reasonable woman who had visited him in his office.

'You knew it wasn't a social call.'

'I knew that, yes. But ask yourself this, Rebecca: what good would it have done to tell you? You would have confronted her and accused her of going behind your back, and that would only have made matters worse.'

'Matters couldn't have got any worse between my mother and myself.'

'Can we forget about this and think about the future?' he pled. 'You've turned your back on your parents and are no longer accepting financial support from them. You're my responsibility now – a responsibility I'm honoured to accept. We have a child arriving and we can't allow the spectres of your parents to keep looming and damaging our relationship.' He tore up her mother's letter and tossed the pieces away. 'Let that be an end to it. No more phone calls, no more letters, no more references to what happened in the past.' He held out his arms to her. 'Don't you see – this is what your mother wants, to cause trouble between us by sending you such a letter? You have to concentrate on your studies and your stained glass work. When the baby arrives I can take care of it, now I'm retired, with time on my hands. I know I have my book to complete, but I'll manage that in the next six months, now that I'm away from meetings and reports.'

He offered to take her to the glass-walled fish restaurant by the sea, but she said that she wasn't hungry, and she went upstairs to the studio. He took her up a mug of coffee at nine, and found her working on a design. He watched the news on television while waiting for her to come down, but when there was no sign of her by eleven he went upstairs and found her in bed, asleep. The way she was occupying the bed made it plain that she wouldn't welcome him beside her, so he went back downstairs again. He drank some whisky and thought of Vivien. Her parents had never caused him any trouble, and the summers they had spent with them on Iona had always been harmonious and stimulating, despite the prayers morning and evening, and at meals.

The art historian yearned for these summers again, packing the car in Edinburgh, where he was a lecturer, driving across to the west coast to catch the ferry to Mull, and then the scenic drive to the short crossing to Iona where they had had the holiday house to themselves. In those days everything had seemed so peaceful and ordered. You never heard talk of global warming, of the sea coming up to doors on Iona. But he was now living in a different world, a world of diminishing choices as he aged. Was it arrogance and an illusion that he could cope with so young a wife, satisfying her not only physically but emotionally as well? She was lying sleeping alone upstairs, obviously still resentful that he had concealed his meeting with her mother. He had discovered a side to her nature that he hadn't seen before in the meek young woman tramping out Bach on the organ in St Salvator's Chapel, or going in under the archway to St Mary's divinity school.

The question which occupied him that night and which was to occupy him on other nights in the future was: had he changed Rebecca by introducing her to the wayward passion of sex? If she had not seen him that night in

St Salvator's, and come down from the organ loft on her swift silent feet to speak with him, would she still be a virgin, having resisted the advances of her fellow male students? Would she still be sitting in her room in McIntosh Hall, reading the classical texts that her father had used when he was at St Andrews University? Or would she have gone into denims in any case in revolt against her parents because of peer pressure? He had seen primly dressed and deferential young students turning into loud-mouthed tykes in the course of a term.

Her husband had to acknowledge to himself that his belief that age had conferred on him the wisdom to understand and to counsel a much younger person was a fallacy. He didn't really understand the desires and frustrations of the young woman lying upstairs, his child growing within her. They had spent much more time having sex than having conversations. The pregnancy was a result.

It was at a time like this that he wished he had firm beliefs like Vivien's parents, and in particular those her minister father had had, when he faced old age and death in the certain knowledge that he would survive in some form, and that he could prepare for the transition in his closing years.

Chapter 16

In the final months of her pregnancy Rebecca, who was now nineteen, seemed to get bigger by the day. She slept by herself and Mackilligin went into the spare room. He felt excluded from her life, though she told him that it was because he was restless in the night and might bump the baby. When she wasn't resting in bed she was studying downstairs or was up in the studio, working on a stained glass design, or else she was along in Jessica Rae's house, receiving more instruction, no longer able to conceal from her teacher than she was pregnant. Mackilligin urged her to invite the few friends she had made in McIntosh Hall to come round to see her, but she said that they hadn't been real friends. When he met his neighbours in the narrow street they didn't stop to chat as they had always done.

His sister-in-law Charlotte wrote to him: 'I understand the student I met you with on Iona is expecting your child. I'm appalled at your behaviour, which is a betrayal of my dear sister. I never want to see or hear from you again.'

He tore up the letter and put it in the bin. The thrill of being able to conceive a child at his age was beginning to be replaced by anxiety about how he would cope with a baby in the house, and especially one for whom he would be the main parent, since Rebecca had become immersed in her stained glass work - at the expense of her university studies, he thought, though he didn't articulate his worry to her. He recalled, when he first visited Vivien's family house on Iona, that Charlotte had just had a baby. Her husband had commandeered the kitchen, immersing the feeding bottles and rubber teats in bowls of hot water to sterilise them while she tested the temperature of the pot of milk on the stove with a thermometer. Was this the ritual he would be getting into, doing the shopping as well, with little time left over for the completion of his book, because he now saw that he had to get a move on before his rival at the Slade published his. Mackilligin was beginning to miss the buzz of academic conferences and wanted to give a series of lectures on his interpretation of Hellenistic statuary, which, he believed, was insightful and new.

But there were too many interruptions to get down to the completion of his book because Rebecca had heavy morning sickness, and it became obvious, through her moaning during the night, when he left the doors of the bedrooms open, that it was going to be a difficult birth. When the contractions started a week before the baby was due he phoned for the doctor, who decided that Rebecca was to be admitted immediately to Ninewells Hospital in Dundee in case of complications because he was worried about the child being born prematurely. The father travelled in the ambulance with her and a paramedic. Rebecca was in great pain, and he held her hand on the half hour ride. He didn't often resort to prayer, but he was doing so on that journey, asking that the child be spared. When they reached Ninewells and she was quickly wheeled away he paced the corridors as the long night began, reflecting on how he had come to be in such a place, in such circumstances. Wouldn't it have been better if he had remained a widower, to have avoided getting into another relationship after his wife's death? But, God willing, he was about to become a father, a state of grace that had eluded him in his marriage, and in what must be the last quarter of his life, was surely a great prize – far greater than publishing an acclaimed book on Hellenistic sculpture.

That September night, when it was still light outside, and the hospital became hushed as most of the staff went home and he awaited the birth, he had plenty of time to review his life. But he didn't want to get too deeply into this retrospection. He had lived his life, however unsatisfactorily in places, and he had to be alert to the future, waiting to hear the cry of a new-born infant from the maternity unit, outside of which he was still pacing, agitated now, because fear had replaced retrospection, and it was mounting into terror. He had squeamishly turned down an invitation to be present at the birth.

Suppose that Rebecca died in childbirth? He would be responsible, because he had seduced her (he couldn't deny this to himself) and made her pregnant. The risks were all on her side. If she died he wouldn't be able to live with himself. His world would collapse and he would have to leave his house with its fond memories.

But if she died, and the baby lived?

Then it would be his responsibility to arrange help to bring it up, with probably a live-in nanny. But as he turned at the end of his agitated strides he had a sinister thought. If he were left a single parent, the grandparents in Edinburgh would try to get custody of their daughter's child. He would fight this with every means at his disposal because he knew now that the grandfather was a ruthless opponent, without mercy.

Four hours after arriving in the hospital he was informed that he was the father of a healthy eight pound daughter, and that his wife was doing well. The nurse led him into the room where the child lay in its mother's arms. The new parent was so overcome that he was lost for words as he put a finger into the tiny hand and kissed his wife.

But there was a complication to them going home to St Andrews. The alterations had been delayed because of a planning backlog, and a house full of hammers, drills and dust wasn't the safest place for a new baby. At considerable expense he had rented a house in one of the wynds in the centre of St Andrews, and had had a cot installed in the second bedroom. He assumed that Rebecca and he would occupy the main bedroom, but she insisted on the cot being moved into that, and because of the lack of space, as well as the feeling that he wasn't wanted, he moved into the second room.

There wasn't time to resume his book. His wife was spending all her time with the child, and he had to do the shopping. As he carried his green bags to the convenient supermarket, he was accosted by Flora Rainsworthy, a colleague from Art History.

'You're a close one, not telling us that you were getting married, and now we hear you have a child.'

'A daughter,' he said, caught by this feisty woman at the counter where he had been selecting organic vegetables for soup.

'And you didn't tell us that your spouse was one of your students.'

'Not really my student,' he corrected her, wishing she would move on with her plastic basket. 'She's studying classics and theology, and only sat in on my lectures when she had time.'

But he could see from this woman's very proximate face (she was an authority on Edvard Munch) that the crime was the same: he had seduced one of his students.

'How is the rewriting of your book coming along?' Flora asked.

'It's difficult finding the time, with the new baby.'

'I bet it is. When I had my first I did no research for a year. There was a big Munch conference in Norway and I had to miss it because I was breast-feeding and unfortunately men aren't equipped in that area to take over. Well, good luck on all fronts.'

Rebecca wasn't breast-feeding, so bottles had to be prepared. Though he fetched the ingredients, she wouldn't let him near the actual process of sterilisation and preparation, at which she seemed to spend hours, with kettles and bowls. Nor was she interested in physical contact. When he came up behind her and put his arms around her, she warned him that 'the stitches they had to put in could give.'

He felt left out of it. Even when he picked up his daughter the mother was there at his back, as if she didn't trust him. He felt old as he held the warm sweet smelling flesh to himself, which didn't seem a part of him, the wrinkles on the face that he had observed at birth now smoothed out by the hand of time for, God willing, a long life, whereas the skin on the back of his hands holding the baby was now gathering in rough folds, as if his body were being prepared for its end. In the mirror of the bathroom cabinet he saw the ugly hairs in his ears, the now permanent lines under his eyes, which looked exhausted, as if they had little vision left in them. The art historian had never been a pessimist, not even in the darkest, most heart-breaking hours of his late wife's malignant illness, when he had lain beside her, wishing he could absorb the fever and the pain. Now he didn't like undressing in front of Rebecca because of the cellulite at his buttocks, the skin on his flank looking as if he had been savaged by a shark while swimming.

Something occurred to him as he stood there, in the rented bathroom, unable to leave his own image in the glass, though it saddened him, a Francis Bacon portrait. Ageing would have been easier to accept if he had been alone. But now his young wife and baby daughter were measures of his own mortality, constant presences that reminded him that he was growing old rapidly, because the clock seemed to have been speeded up after sixty. He had to live on, to keep healthy and lucid for their sake, because they depended on him - at least financially. That morning, as his breath clouded the bathroom mirror, he calculated that when he was eighty, his daughter would be eighteen, and by that stage (if he were still alive), he would not be able to keep up with the energy and optimism of youth.

These were depressing thoughts, and he saw the tears in his own eyes before his breath on the glass obscured his face, and he went through to answer his young wife's summons. Another nappy had to be disposed of, wrapped up so that it wouldn't smell when conveyed out to the bin, and then it was time to go to his house, to check on the progress of the alterations. When would the work be finished? The man pushed back his hard yellow hat and scratched his sweated brow. They had hit a snag.

'What is it?' the client asked apprehensively.

'This lintel,' the worker said, indicating the one above the bedroom being altered. He tapped the slab with the pencil pulled from behind his ear.

'What about it?'

'Well, when we were about to reinforce it the architect came in and made us stop.'

'For safety reasons?' he asked.

'Not for safety reasons. Because it's a grave slab.'

'How did a grave slab get into a house?' Mackilligin wanted to know.

'You've to phone the architect.'

He was reminded of what Ronald Cant the town historian had told him: after St Andrews Cathedral was wrecked in the Reformation, the citizens had helped themselves to the stonework.

'You appear to have in your house a grave slab from the Cathedral; at least that's what it looks like,' the architect informed him. 'I have a duty to inform Historic Scotland, and one of their inspectors is coming to see it tomorrow afternoon. Can you make it at three?'

He did his shopping early and was there at the appointed hour. The inspector had a digital camera with him to photograph the slab.

'Am I going to have to leave it exposed and allow the public to come trooping in to see it?' Mackilligin asked in exasperation.

'Of course you don't have to open your house to the public. And we aren't going to remove this lintel and place it in the museum in the Cathedral grounds. This is where it belongs after all these years.'

But when the inspector went away the builder had bad news.

'We've found a beam riddled with dry rot. We can't just remove it, otherwise the masonry above it will come crashing down and maybe bring part of the roof with it because it's a load-bearing structure. We'll have to use props to hold up the stonework while we get the beam out.'

'How long is this going to take?' Mackilligin asked truculently.

'A week, I'd say.'

Mackilligin was in a furious mood at the delay this would mean as he tramped back to the rented flat, swearing audibly that nothing was going right in his life. He was still only at the first chapter of his rewritten book, and even then it didn't flow like its predecessor destroyed in the rugby referee's rampage. His wife would hardly let him near his child, and certainly not near her body. He could feel the pressure building up to a dangerous level in his ageing arteries as he went in to dispose of another shitty nappy, and to cook the supper in a confined kitchen where most of the work surface seemed to be taken up by the bottles and tins of the baby milk producing plant operated by his wife.

'They've found a rotten beam, so that'll mean a delay of a week,' he informed his wife as he tenderised the steaks.

'That's all I need,' she complained. 'I want to get the baby settled in her own room. This place isn't infant-friendly. It's an old person's house.'

If she became aware of what she had just said, she didn't show it, but went on measuring out exactly the ingredients for the evening feed which she couldn't provide herself. He was deeply wounded, the pain greater than he would have sustained if the blade he was using to trim the fat from the steaks had gone into his thumb. He felt cornered by life, alone, vulnerable, old. It was an explosive moment in which all his pent-up frustration and resentment could have poured out. But he had sufficient instinct to know that if this happened, she would quit the house with their child, because she had the fiercely protective – and ultimately ruthless – instincts of the new mother. He had to remember that there were now three of them.

The bills for the renovation work had started coming in, and there were extras he hadn't anticipated – wormed floorboards that had to be replaced, lethal electrics exposed, the rotten beam. After he had washed the grease from the supper dishes and utensils he sat at the two-person table in the corner of the kitchen to write out cheques. He saw his lump sum diminishing, his university pension being swallowed up by the expenses of a child. Counting the damage on the cheque stubs was too depressing, so he went through for his laptop and tried to resume his book. But the baby was querulous, the mother trying to subdue her with a song. It should have been a magical moment, with the window opened to the balmy autumn evening, but the lullaby didn't have a healing effect on this father's heart. He was beginning to feel the strain of fatherhood, to realise that he didn't have the energy to cope with an infant, and at the same time complete his book. But he had made his choice and the child had to take priority whenever she cried, or was due her feed.

Through in the bedroom the singing was having the desired effect, and when the child was sleeping Rebecca switched on the night-light in the shape of a duck, its pink glow suffusing the room. She left the door open and went down to the sitting-room which she had turned into her study. She had a translation from Sappho to make for the following day, but found the Greek flowing easily because of her sense of fulfilment at being a mother. She stopped after two stanzas, her pen resting against her teeth as she reflected that, really, a new mother didn't need a husband – except for practical reasons. The emotional bond was exclusive and totally sufficient. At this point she felt that she wouldn't miss sex if she never went to bed with her husband again. The stitches were an excuse to keep him at bay: the pain had put her off intercourse, which now seemed like an invasion.

Before she resumed her Sappho translation she thought

about her parents. Motherhood was making her more tolerant towards them. Of course the umpire shouldn't have beaten up the father of her child, and of course her mother shouldn't have tried to dictate adoption. But sitting in Santa Chiara in Assisi, listening to the unseen nuns singing Vespers with a sweetness and sincerity to die for, Rebecca had realised that she was lacking tolerance towards her parents. Christ had talked a lot about forgiveness. Shouldn't she forgive her mother, practise charity towards her? Shouldn't she be invited to see her grandchild, not, of course, in St Andrews, because that would upset Alan? But when the wee girl was older and able to travel, she could be taken to the Morningside villa, where they might even stay overnight.

Rebecca's benevolent thoughts came out of the conviction that her parents couldn't harm her now, and she wondered, before she resumed the Sappho translation that was proving surprisingly easy, if she shouldn't name the baby Felicity, after her mother? The name, which meant happiness, had a pleasant sound.

Chapter 17

The Mackilligins were back in their own house, at last. The new nursery had been decorated white, and there was new furniture. Rebecca loved the room, but couldn't spend as much time as she would have liked with their child because she had to catch up on her studies. Besides, she wanted to devote time to her stained glass education. While Mackilligin watched the baby below she worked in the studio of her predecessor, developing a design for her first piece of stained glass work. Jessica Rae had told her about the importance of structure in the disposition of the lines of lead in the design.

"'It's like life itself," Rebecca reported the elderly artist as cautioning her. "If you have too many lead lines intersecting at the one point, that makes for a weak design, with the eye drawn to this one place instead of to the whole picture. And if your design contains too many long vertical or horizontal lead lines, then the structure is weakened, and the eye isn't satisfied.'"

Her first stained glass piece had evolved from doodles, and she was now working on a scaled sketch, using a box of watercolours. Jessica had explained that the next part of the careful process ('nothing should be rushed') was to enlarge the sketch to a full-sized drawing ('called a cartoon, my dear'). Then she was to make two copies of the cartoon, using carbon tracing paper. She was still a long way from reaching for the first tool from Vivien's rack, but she found the design process therapeutic as she sat painting in the colours on the scaled sketch.

Downstairs, Mackilligin was trying to advance his book while the baby slept in the carrycot which he had placed beside the sofa where he was sitting hunched over the laptop. But he couldn't concentrate, though the child was sleeping peacefully. He had paid the builders' last account that morning, making a sizeable hole in his retirement lump sum. His pension, once seen as substantial, wasn't going far with all the new expenses, the bulky packets of disposable nappies he lugged home from Boots, the top-of-the-range baby food that Rebecca insisted on; food for themselves, high quality organic; the extra electricity; books; the incidentals that added up. They were eating into capital at an alarming rate.

He found that the strain of running a house with three people in it was making him forgetful. It wasn't only the mislaying of the car keys, the title of a book forgotten as he searched his shelves upstairs: he found that he was forgetting the names of Hellenistic statues as he struggled to recreate his book. He was also having palpitations, and as he lay in bed alone, he could hear his heart sounding. He wondered if he should take his worries to his doctor, but he knew that there was no physical basis to his symptoms and that he would be given tranquillizers, which would dull his perceptions. It was essential to keep going, to be fit and healthy mentally as well as physically to meet his obligations to his wife and child, and to his book, too long in the birth process.

'You forgot to put salt in the potatoes,' Rebecca criticised him when she came down for the supper he had cooked.

'I'm sorry. My mind was on other matters. My book isn't going too well.'

'Why not?' she asked in a tone that wasn't full of concern.

'I don't know. I suppose that the first one – the one your father destroyed – was written in the heat of inspiration. I don't seem to be able to retrieve these insights.'

'We need to think about having the baby christened. I want to call her Felicity.'

'But that's your mother's name,' he responded in astonishment. 'Your sworn enemy. You can't want your daughter to be burdened with that name, after all that bitch has put you through.'

'My mother doesn't own the name, Alan.'

He had let other provocations go for the sake of peace, but this one had to be met head-on, otherwise their daughter would be saddled with a name which he despised. He wanted to call his daughter Virginia, after his mother.

'How can your forgive her cruelty?' he challenged his wife.

'I have to.'

'You have to?' he raised his voice. 'Why do you have to? She's the wife of the man who attacked me, remember. She probably sent him here to sort me out.'

'I doubt that,' Rebecca said quietly.

'Why do you doubt it?'

'You're raising your voice: remember the baby.'

But he had started, and he couldn't cap the well of resentment and tension that came shooting out. He was deaf to the volume of his own voice as he told her that her parents were the worst people he had ever met.

'Are you quite finished?' she asked with the same calmness.

'As a matter of fact no!' he spelt out his opposition in a series of thumps to the table. 'I will not have my daughter called Felicity.'

'She's my daughter too.'

'Our daughter,' he corrected her. 'This should be a democratic decision. What I need to know is: how have you come to this charitable revision of your opinion of your parents, whom, as I remember, you hated?'

She wasn't going to enlighten him that it was while sitting in the Santa Chiara Basilica in Assisi she had realised, filled as she had been with a feeling of exultation, that one had to forgive. It had been a strange experience, as if she had seen her mother standing in front of the altar in her designer clothes and sculpted hair, her crocodile skin handbag on her arm, staring at her daughter. The lesson that Rebecca had carried away from Assisi – as carefully as the blue wall tile with the raised relief of St Francis feeding the birds, wrapped in her nightdress – was that in order to make spiritual progress, and to achieve calmness and insight in life, one had to forgive, no matter the extent of the sin. The vision standing in front of the altar, clothed by Jenners, shod by Gamba on high thin heels, was asking for her forgiveness.

'I want the baby to be called Felicity. I want to start a process of forgiveness.'

Mackilligin started laughing, as if he had cracked. So he had suffered the battering fists and the thudding brogue of the rugby referee for nothing? So he, who was providing the home and the money to support her, and who was the father of the child, was to have no say in her naming?

That was when the unnamed baby woke up and began crying, when the mother lost her temper as he laughed, his head thrown back, his weight braced on his spread fingers on the pine table, among the ruins of the meal, the fresh haddock not touched on either plate.

'You're a brute!' she hissed as she hugged the baby close before carrying her up to the sanctuary of the bedroom.

He sank down, head in his hands. Was this despair or anger? It was both, two emotions that are an explosive mix. He felt that he wanted to wreck the kitchen, as his assailant from Edinburgh had done. But what good would that do, when he would have to clean up the debris? To whom were his mixed emotions directed? Against his second wife, for her exclusion of him from the naming process of their child? This was the rock-bottom despair of a man who felt that his penis, which should have been quiescent at his age, had led him into this mess, which he wasn't even going to begin to detail in his head, but which included responsibilities to a young wife and child, and money worries.

He felt like running out, but where was he going to go to? To another town, far from Fife, to set up a modest place for himself? But he knew that that wasn't practical. He would have rent to pay, and would also have to support the St Andrews house and his wife and child. He knew that he couldn't afford two properties. He knew that he had to stay to try to prevent his life from deteriorating any further. But it was going to have to be a process of appeasement, because Rebecca was no longer the quiet timid girl in outdated clothes he had first met in St Salvator's Chapel. She had developed into a formidable woman, ready to give as good as she got. She had matured remarkably – and perhaps excessively – within a year.

Vivien had been gentle and considerate, the calm contemplation of her work as a stained glass artist transferred to her life. She had laid out the holistic cutting pattern, and her touch was sure and careful as she cut the glass with the wheeled tool. She knew that the lead had to be stretched carefully, the channel to receive the glass opened up with a sure hand with the lathekin, which she had shaped herself, from a piece of hardwood. She knew how carefully the glass pieces had to be fitted in, and when she came down from her studio after the day's work she brought her satisfaction and peace of mind as a gift for him, intangible but felt and appreciated as he sat opposite her, eating the healthy food she had prepared with the same respect she had accorded to the glass, fanning out the organic lettuce under the sparkling tap, splitting the tomato, grown without poisonous chemicals, into two coronets for their blue plates. Everything Vivien had done was measured, calm, even fitting him inside her, as if there were no hurry, not wishing to diminish or destroy the pleasure through haste.

Vivien had been religious, hardly surprising in an artist

whose speciality was stained glass windows for churches. She prayed in solitude in her studio, before soldering the panel, fixing the pattern, and she said grace over her salads. But she didn't force her beliefs down his throat.

But this second wife was different. To her husband it was as if she had picked up religion, like malaria, in the stifling streets of Assisi, as if she had been bitten and infected, her brain affected, sitting in the dim – and to him, depressing – Basilica of Santa Chiara, listening to the nuns chanting. If she could have taken the Host in every church they went into, she would have. It seemed to him that she was developing religious mania, compensating for her cruel and loveless upbringing by finding refuge in Catholicism, the religion that her mother had perverted. But this was as far as he could go in his analysis of his wife's psychological state, because she refused to discuss her feelings with him, and because he wasn't a devout person himself. God was fine, in His place, to be appealed to in times of stress and grief, but not an all-pervading presence in his life. He could take or leave Him, like certain vegetables.

Upstairs, while her husband was in anguish, Rebecca was kneeling by her bed with her quietened child, praying for guidance. She didn't know how to handle the tempestuous man below, who seemed to have changed drastically since she first came to his house and ascended the stairs in front of him to be deflowered. She was asking for help to find the road ahead as she knelt by her sleeping infant, an image which one of the Flemish masters would have turned into a breath-stopping study of the Madonna and Child, because the scene was ancient despite the modern décor, the chipboard on the walls, the furniture made out of sawdust and glue.

She was in despair. She was too young, too inexperienced to handle a sixty plus man whom she heard rising several times in the night for the toilet, his prostate weakening. She had lost interest in sex with him, not only because she had been stretched and stitched in the process of giving birth, but because she found his body unappealing, the member losing its rigidity, the offensive tinge to his breath as if he had feasted on garlic, and when he padded away to the bathroom, she saw the marks on the buttocks as though he had been flogged.

Did this mean that she was judging her husband from his physical deterioration and didn't love him? This was the hardest part to decide, the part she wanted guidance for through prayer. What was love? Was the love she was supposed to have for her husband the same love that she showed towards the child sleeping peacefully on her bed? But surely these were two distinct loves, she reasoned on her knees, because her love for her husband came with physical demands and obligations, whereas her love for this baby was unconditional. Yes, the physical attention of a child was important, but it was different, purer, less demanding than the physical attention to – and from – a man. The love for a child was spontaneous, without coarseness, the fulfilment in the act of holding, of feeding, of soothing.

She would go to sleep with these anxieties, lying on the bed beside her child, and when she woke it was ten o'clock.

She lay listening, but the house seemed to be in silence. Had he gone to bed? She rose, cautiously, laid the baby in her cot and went out on to the landing. She stood with head bowed outside his door, but couldn't hear his characteristic snoring, as if there were an animal in the room with him. She went down the stairs cautiously, holding on to the banister. She walked bare-footed along the tiled passage and into the kitchen cum sitting-room.

The dishes from the aborted supper had been washed by hand and stacked in the slotted plastic rack to dry. The rejected haddock was lying on a plate, covered in cling-film against the lingering flies of late autumn, to be fed to the neighbour's cat come morning. The house was therapeutically silent. But where was he?

Then she saw him, in the shadows, lying stretched out on the sofa. At first she feared that he had died of a stroke after their argument over the naming of their child, but when she stood over him she saw his lips pursing in sleep. She studied him, as if he were to be the subject of a painting, or even a stained glass panel. He looked old and vulnerable, as if he had aged dramatically in the course of that unhappy day. His chest under the green sweater rose and fell as if there were problems with his lungs. He looked as if he were confronting a frightening presence in his sleep. She studied his face, and for a moment wanted to fetch a pair of scissors to clip those straggling eyebrows.

This was an old face, a face that had had most of its time. From the perspective of youth she found it difficult, if not impossible, to understand the concept of ageing. She knew that there was much more to it than physical deterioration, exhausted skin, rheumy eyes, a back bowed as the muscles gave way. But she didn't, couldn't appreciate what was going on inside the head of this sleeping sexagenarian, her husband, though tonight she could see the agitation of his dreams in his face. How did a person who had lived so long, and couldn't expect the same length again, view the future? With terror or composure? Her Catholic education had informed her that ageing was an inevitable process, not to be feared, but to be respected, even cherished, because it wasn't the end of life, but the approach to an eternal state in which the aged body with its broken veins and brittle bones would be redundant.

She remembered the afternoon when she had tried to read the future in his sleeping face in the hotel in Glasgow, asking herself if she were going to be saddled with a man who would become an invalid. Now, his wife and mother of his child, she was trying to look for the spirit in the face of this man stretched out on the sofa in their St Andrews home, but his eyes were closed. Then, as she stood there, in the silence of night, she saw his expression change. He was smiling now. What welcome presence had entered his sleep, replacing the sinister, she wondered? Was he dreaming about her? She wanted to think so, as she remained there, hearing the rhythmic rising and falling of his breathing. If she were going to forgive her mother, then she was also going to have to forgive her husband. It was with this compassionate thought that Rebecca noticed that he was smiling because he had an erection. Only a few months before she would have welcomed this, but now she felt disgusted. If she were the stimulus for this arousal, was this what he thought of her, as a sex object?

Mackilligin opened his eyes and saw what he took to be a terrifying apparition of his wife.

He felt that he needed to get away from St Andrews for the day, so he told Rebecca that he was going to Edinburgh to do more research for his book. He was wandering aimlessly along Princes Street when his sleeve was tugged, and he turned to see Grace Armstrong, who had been in the fine art degree course at Edinburgh with Vivien and himself.

They embraced with loud greetings. She had been a striking looking student, and though her red hair had turned grey, she was still attractive. She had been a close friend of Vivien's, but though they exchanged cards at Christmas they hadn't met since university days, since Grace had gone on from Edinburgh to do a doctorate in London. Her speciality was the Bloomsbury group of painters, and in particular Dora Carrington. The book she had written on them had appeared at a time when there was a resurgence of interest in Bloomsbury, and on the strength of it she had been invited to America. He saw notification of her publications and honours from time to time in arts journals, and knew that she was a professor at Harvard.

'I'm fine, but how are *you*? I was so sorry to hear about Vivien's death. Did you get the wreath I sent?'

It was a tacit rebuke to him for not acknowledging it, and he duly apologised.

'I've remarried.'

'Well congratulations!' she said, kissing him on the cheek. 'Is it someone from the arts world?'

'I married one of my students.'

He saw the surprise and alarm in her attractive face.

'A mature student?'

'No, not mature.'

Grace had always been forthright, which was probably why she had such a successful academic career across the Atlantic.

'But the age gap must be huge.'

'It's big,' he confessed. 'But that doesn't mean that a relationship won't work. In fact we have a child.'

A gloved hand went to her cheek as if an insect had bitten her.

'What were you thinking of, Alan?'

'I was lonely after Vivien's death, and Rebecca was very sympathetic.'

'What age is your wife, Alan?'

'Nineteen.'

She shook her head. 'I can't believe you would do this. I don't mean that it's a betrayal of Vivien, but think of the strain it must be putting on your life at an age when you should be a grandfather, not a new parent. I've waited for years for the appearance of your book on Hellenistic sculpture. Have I somehow missed its publication?'

He shook his head sadly.

'But you've been working on this book for years and years, Alan. What's happened?'

'I had heavy commitments at St Andrews.'

'But you were surely entitled to a sabbatical.'

'I did get one, but didn't make the progress I expected to make.'

'You're not going to finish it now, with a baby to look after.'

'I will, now that I've retired. What about you?'

'I'm going to go on until Harvard tells me that it's time to retire. I'd miss the teaching. Wouldn't it have been better to have stayed on at St Andrews to finish your book? I mean, you're off the academic circuit now, and it may be difficult for you to promote it through conferences. I was going to invite you to Harvard to give us a seminar.'

The small immaculately dressed woman was beginning to irritate him, but also to make him envious. Hers had been an exemplary academic career. She had never married, but she didn't look forlorn. She had worn better than he had, and still felt that she had a contribution to make to art scholarship. She told him that she was visiting relatives in Edinburgh, but would be returning to the States the following week, for a conference on Carrington and Bloomsbury which she was hosting at Harvard.

'You must finish your book, Alan, baby or no baby,' she urged him. 'Remember that this is what Vivien would have wanted. She had such faith in you, and so did I. The trouble is, the academic world is so competitive, and if you delay the publication of a book by too long, you get pre-empted by some smart young academic. Finish your book and I'll arrange a seminar at Harvard. You can stay with me for a few days. I have a very nice apartment, with a peaceful view. You can get away by yourself, can't you?'

'I'm sure I can.'

'I often think of those days at university when you, Vivien and I talked so earnestly about art. We were living in the age of Warhol's trash, but we still managed to preserve standards.'

Chapter 18

As he pushed the buggy through the historic wynds of St Andrews Mackilligin had the encounter he dreaded when he met one of his third year students.

'Is this your grandchild?' she enquired as she bent over the sleeping infant.

'She's my daughter and this is my wife Rebecca,' he was forced to make the introduction, but saw in the student's face surprise and scepticism. The baby was no longer a sign of his virility, but of the marked age difference between the parents. When he saw a colleague approaching he steered the cumbersome buggy down another wynd.

The atmosphere seemed full of tension, as if his nerves were being stretched, like the lead calmes in the vice Rebecca had clamped to make her first piece of stained glass work. She had followed the procedure which Jessica Rae had instructed, slipping a sheet of paper, about the weight of wrapping paper, under the completed cartoon. Then a sheet of heavier kraft paper was placed under the wrapping paper. 'Place your carbon paper face down between these sheets,' Jessica had instructed her apprentice. 'You'll need to secure this assembly of paper, so that they don't shift around while you're tracing. I use tape for this purpose. You need to use a hard pencil to trace down the centre of your heavy lead lines. Remember, you need only one line to follow when cutting your pattern and assembling the glass and lead.'

Rebecca was working in the studio when she heard him

shouting. She hurried out of the studio and up the stairs and saw him bending over the cot.

'What's wrong?'

The baby in his arms was a blue colour.

'Phone the doctor!' she screamed at him as she put her mouth to the child's.

He dropped the phone and it skidded under the sofa. He retrieved it on his hands and knees. He phoned 999 and seemed to have to hold on for ages in his desperation. The operator tried to make him coherent, to make him give his address.

'We need a doctor and an ambulance for our baby!'

He was too terrified to go upstairs again, so he stood by the open door, looking up and down the street, beginning to imagine that he had fallen asleep on the sofa and that this was a terrible dream. He heard the ambulance before he saw it, but because of cars parked on the pavement it couldn't get down the narrow street.

'Where's the baby?' the paramedics asked him.

He pointed upwards and heard their rapid feet ascending. He went down on his knees on the cobbles and began to pray, more intensely than he had ever prayed in his life. 'Dear God, let Felicity be all right.' He had reluctantly agreed the name for the christening, which had been arranged for the week before Christmas. He was still on his knees on the cobbles when he heard the commotion behind him. One of the paramedics was struggling with Rebecca, but she beat him away.

'You didn't watch her!'

Still on his knees, he protected his bowed head with his crossed arms as the blows rained down and she kicked him on the side. He couldn't be helped to his feet by the paramedic because he was trying to restrain the distraught mother, so he had to crawl back into his house, along the passage like a wounded animal, watched by fearful neighbours who had come out at the disturbance. The other paramedic was upstairs with the baby, phoning for a doctor. When he came downstairs he was shaking his head, and the bereaved mother started screaming again, snatching at whatever was within reach and throwing it at her husband.

'You killed my baby!'

She picked up his laptop and held it above her head with both hands, then heaved it towards him. As it struck the side of his head the screen shattered, cutting him.

'It may be better if you take him out of here,' the doctor advised one of the paramedics, who led Mackilligin out to the ambulance and helped him into the back, where he attended to the superficial wound on the side of his face.

'What killed her?' he asked, sobbing.

'I don't know, sir. That's a matter for the doctor.'

'But I did look in to see that she was all right.'

Even as he said this, he wasn't sure that it was accurate. He had been rewriting his Hellenistic book on the laptop and hadn't attended to the clock. His thought processes had been flowing fluently, and he was finding the expressive language that had gone with the damaged disk of his first laptop as he wrote about the Venus de Milo. Had fifteen, twenty minutes passed before he had gone upstairs to look round the door? Or could it have been as much as an hour? He didn't know because he was in shock. From now on Rebecca would blame him and hate him, even though he had fulfilled his duty of looking after their child while she cut out her stained glass pattern. How could he live with himself if it had been longer?

The doctor decided to move Rebecca from the house to the local hospital so that she could be sedated, but she braced her hands against the door-posts as she was helped out, shouting that she wasn't going to leave her baby.

'She hasn't been christened! She can't go into limbo!'

The police came to check out the tragedy, and then the body was removed in the ambulance. Mackilligin was alone in the empty house, but it seemed to him to have become an alien, hostile place. He went upstairs to the bedroom and saw the depression in the bed where the paramedics had worked desperately, trying to get the tiny heart going again. He took the blanket from the cot and stuffed its fragrance into his wailing mouth. The room seemed to be going round him, and he had to hold on to the side of the cot to prevent himself falling into the black hole that his mind had become.

If there had been pills in the house he would probably have swallowed them, but he went downstairs and threw away the cap of a choice malt whisky bottle that he had been keeping for esteemed visitors. He didn't use a glass and it dribbled down his chin, drinking three quarters of it before he crashed out unconscious on the sofa.

In the course of the next two days he drank everything in the house that he could lay hands on. He didn't shed his clothes or go for a shower, nor did he prepare food for himself. He needed to maintain the oblivion of alcohol, because to crawl back out of it into reality meant that he would have to face the terrible tragedy, that the child, born to an elderly man and therefore loved to adoration, was dead. His wife would never return to him. He would have to leave this house with its memories of the deaths of loved ones, to try to establish a new life beyond St Andrews. But he knew that he was too old to do this with fulfilment and contrition.

On the third day Rebecca was standing over the sofa, shaking him awake.

'Felicity has to be laid to rest.'

He thought that she was telling him to carry the tired child up to her cot, until he came round to the realisation of what she was saying. The light was cruel to his eyes, and she looked twice her age, her face wasted with grief.

'I am so sorry,' he whispered, 'so very very sorry.'

She pushed an empty whisky bottle with her toe and it rolled under the sofa.

'They think it was a cot death.'

'It was still my fault. I should have been more vigilant.'

She shook her head.

'They don't know what causes cot deaths. Some doctors say that the baby turns over on to its face and smothers itself. It wasn't your fault. It was an act of God.'

But he would never believe otherwise.

'We have to go on,' she told him tenderly as she helped him up. She arranged a Mass for the baby and when the priest had shaken holy water over the small white coffin Mackilligin picked it up and carried it in his arms out to the open hearse. Ten of his colleagues had turned up at the cemetery on the warm morning and he was grateful for their hugs and handshakes before the earth trickled through his fingers on to the white shape beyond his shoes. That afternoon Rebecca climbed back up to the studio. She loaded the brush with bright colours from the enamel box and began to paint another design. He padded across from the shower, his hair sleeked, and laid his hand on his wife's shoulder.

'We can try for another baby.'

She laid her cheek against his hand and said nothing.

He carried his damaged laptop round to IT Services.

'You're beginning to make a habit of this,' the technician who had condemned his first laptop warned him.

'I fell down the stairs again.'

'Time to move to a bungalow. My mother did that and loves it.'

He didn't want to be reminded of his age as he watched the technician extracting the hard disk with the delicacy of a surgeon removing a vital organ. When he came back a few days later the technician told him: 'you're very lucky. I've managed to save the data and transfer it to one of our servers. When you get yourself a new computer, come and see me and I'll give you your stuff on a CD. I'd advise a desktop. You can't fall down stairs with that.'

For both of the bereaved parents the house was a sad place without the baby.

'We should move,' he advised Rebecca when they were eating supper.

'No. That would be running away. We have to stay and turn our grief into something positive. I like the studio here. You must try to get on with your book. You told me that someone at the Slade is working on the same topic, and you don't want to be pre-empted after all those years.'

But he couldn't concentrate as he sat on the sofa with his new laptop, working on the chapter that the technician had saved for him. He kept lifting his head from the screen, as if listening for a baby crying. He had tried making advances to Rebecca in the bed he was sharing with her again, but she told him that she 'wasn't ready.' He lay thinking that she didn't want another baby, whereas he did, desperately. With the bereavement he felt himself ageing drastically, his own face shocking him in the bathroom mirror, the skin tightening to show up the bone structure beneath. When Rebecca eventually let him lift her nightdress it was a miserable failure on his part. He couldn't bring himself to propose artificial insemination, because that signalled the failure of his manhood, the victory of age.

Two days later he answered the door. Immaculately dressed, Felicity Campbell-Arthurson was standing, extending a gloved hand.

'I had to come to tell you how sorry I am about the baby.'

He didn't shake her hand. 'My wife won't see you,' he warned her.

But Rebecca was behind him. She pushed him aside and embraced her mother.

'How do you know about the baby?' she asked.

'A friend in St Andrews phoned to tell me. She said that she had never seen anything so moving in her life as your husband carrying that tiny white coffin down the aisle after the funeral Mass. She said – she's a clever woman, who studied English here – that it was as if his own broken heart was inside the box.'

'It was God's will, mother.'

'You must be finding support in your faith, dear.'

'I am, and through my work.'

'Your work?' her mother asked, puzzled.

'I'm working with stained glass now.'

'I'm so glad we've found each other again.'

'We were going to call the baby after you.'

Mackilligin was getting angry as he followed them into the kitchen. What was going on? This was the young woman who had condemned her mother for her emotional coldness and control and whose husband had beaten him up. Yet here she was, talking animatedly with her and making her tea. He felt excluded and knew that he might not be able to hold back berating this unwelcome caller.

'I'm so sorry about your loss,' his mother-in-law commiserated with him as they moved through to the lounge.

He shrugged and turned to leave.

'Mother's come to make things up,' Rebecca rebuked him.

'I'm not interested.'

'What has she done to you?' his wife flared up.

'She fucked up your life.'

Felicity closed her eyes, but remained straight-spined on the sofa. He saw that he was going to have to physically throw her out.

'She's come here in a spirit of reconciliation,' Rebecca continued. 'Can't you see that she's genuinely sorry about the loss of the baby?'

He grunted, and sat down at a distance from his adversary.

'Your husband came up here and beat me up.'

Felicity put a gloved hand over her mouth as if to stifle nausea.

'It's true,' her daughter nodded. 'He could have killed Alan. At the time I wanted to have the police charge him, but Alan wouldn't let me. And he smashed Alan's laptop containing the book he was writing.'

Felicity shook her head sadly. 'I knew nothing of this. I have a husband who doesn't confide in me. He doesn't communicate except to issue orders. I've seen more of the back page of the Telegraph than I've seen of his face in twenty five years of marriage.'

'Does he know you're here?' their daughter enquired.

'Oh God no. He would go off his head. He thinks your husband is the devil incarnate. You have a father who never makes peace, Rebecca. Not that I'm blameless myself. I've been too selfish, too preoccupied with material things that don't matter, too taken up with shallow friends. It took the death of your child to show me the error of my ways, which is why I need to be forgiven – by both of you.'

'I forgive you,' Rebecca said, moving to sit beside her on the sofa, putting her arm round the fitted shoulders.

'I think we should go out for a meal – my treat,' Felicity announced.

'That would be nice,' her daughter agreed.

Mackilligin was weary and didn't have the stomach for an argument with this woman who, he had to admit to himself, he was intimidated by, and also impressed by, the way she maintained her composure and her posture. He couldn't decide if her repentance for her heartlessness towards her daughter was genuine, or a ruse to get into their lives and cause more trouble. He was on edge because the book was going so badly that he was considering abandoning it, though he knew that would remove one of the major driving forces of his existence. His inability to maintain an erection on the rare occasions when he was allowed to approach Rebecca in bed was a source of shame. He had gone on websites to see what stimulating aids were available to the man with potency problems. Though tempted by an offer from a Canadian pharmacy to ship him a supply of Viagra, he decided that taking the drug was too dangerous in his present state of mind.

His mother-in-law took them to the glass-walled Seafood Restaurant and invited them to have the run of the menu. But he wasn't hungry and only ordered a smoked salmon starter, avoiding looking at his mother-in-law by staring out of the panoramic window towards the ocean rolling up on the glistening sand where birds were walking. He wondered if having another child would be the solution to the problems between himself and his wife, who was talking animatedly with her mother about the spiritual uplift she had experienced in Assisi.

'I would love to go there with you – at my expense, of course,' Felicity said.

Mackilligin made no attempt to enter the conversation, and knew that he wasn't wanted. Mother and daughter had a lot of catching up to do, a lot of affection to generate, and he had no part in this reconciliation because he was a comparative newcomer into their lives. The problem probably wasn't the lack of a child but his increasing awareness that he was ageing more rapidly than he had anticipated. He had thought that in retirement the advent of old age would be a slow and gentle process, allowing him time for leisure and enjoyment, until he had to acknowledge finally that he was exhausted. Suppose that he had never met Rebecca and was living alone, dining occasionally in quality restaurants in St Andrews and taking holidays abroad to escape the East Neuk winter? As he became less able to look after himself he would have hired a home help, and then, when it was obvious that he couldn't be left with a gas cooker and steep stairs, he would probably have gone into a nursing home.

'Are you sure you won't have more than that, Alan?'

He was jerked out of his reverie by his mother-in-law's voice, addressing him in the tone she would use for a child.

'No thanks,' he replied too abruptly.

The two women finished with a concoction of palate-cleansing sorbets, and then Rebecca asked him to drive her mother to the train. The females sat in the back chatting, and had a long hug at the station before the train pulled away with their visitor.

'That was a pleasant surprise,' Rebecca said as he drove home.

'Does a leopard change its spots?'

'That's unfair, Alan. It must have taken a lot of courage for her to come here to apologise. Mother's always been a proud woman.'

'So the years of emotional cruelty are wiped out, are they?' he wanted to know.

'We have to forgive and forget.'

'I can't forget that your father beat me up.'

'She told you, she didn't know. And she didn't tell him that she was coming here today. Can't you see that she's the way she is because she's dominated by him?'

'That particular deduction isn't in the psychology books I've read, Rebecca,' he observed as they approached St Andrews, where he had once been so happy and fulfilled.

Chapter 19

Mackilligin had always looked forward to the return of the university students after the vacations because they represented youth and vitality, but this time he resented having to step off the pavement as they approached, and the long queues in the supermarket irritated him as he manoeuvred the laden trolley. At home he was deprived of his wife's company because of the hours she was spending, preparing the design in the studio.

'What about your studies?' he asked.

'I don't think I'm going to go back to them.'

'Why not?' He was dismayed, having hoped that when she graduated she would contribute to the household funds.

'I'm bored with the subjects.'

'But you're a religious person,' he reminded her, baffled.

'Yes, but what they study in theology is very different from what I believe in. I want to concentrate on my stained glass work. Jessica thinks that I can make a living out of it through commissions.'

This decision was a blow to him. He was already subsidising the household from his capital, and the interest on what was left was diminishing each month because of the global volatility of the stock market, a worldwide recession looming, the bankers walking away with loaded pockets.

Something else was worrying him. As he struggled to resume his magnum opus he noticed that the words he had in mind weren't the words he typed. Was this because he was under strain? He opened up Google to see if he could find an explanation for the frightening phenomenon. He was directed to a website which informed him that Terry Pratchett, the famous writer of fantasy, had discovered, after a minor stroke, that what he was typing didn't make sense. 'I have been diagnosed with Early Onset Alzheimer's,' Pratchett wrote.

Mackilligin experienced terrible fear as he read this revelation. This was what had happened to his mother. The sweet lady had had to be put into a nursing home. Always so fastidious about her person, the former nurse had wet the chair, and used the f- word frequently and with force as she struck out at her helpers.

Her son shut down his laptop and went for a walk along the sands to try to come to terms with this vision of his future. The symptoms were already showing on the screen, penis instead of Venus. He knew in his heart (sometimes a more reliable indicator than the head) that he had the condition. He didn't want to go for a brain scan, to be shown the deterioration. He had read somewhere that if a person maintained their intellectual interests after retirement, they were less likely to develop dementia than others less active and involved mentally. But he hadn't done this to the same extent that would have happened if he hadn't become involved with Rebecca.

How was he going to be able to tell her that she was to be burdened with a husband for whom senility had already commenced, and for whom dementia now seemed a certain prospect? He knew that the emotional bond between them – and perhaps even the respect – wasn't strong enough to allow her to dedicate herself to his wellbeing, vigilant that he wouldn't go head-first down the stairs, watchful that he wouldn't be found wandering the town, no longer recognising his bearings. She wouldn't be his keeper because she had become absorbed in stained glass work and had probably found her vocation. His mother had had to wear a nappy. Was he to become Rebecca's second baby?

It wasn't a question of making a decision, he knew, as he turned at the curve of the sands, putting up a flock of plovers, like gold coins thrown at the sun. The spires and towers of the town he had come to love were in front of him, but now seemed a long way off, as if he were never going to reach it, even with his long stride. Had it been a mistake to have stayed in this appealing place with its bracing atmosphere, its palpable history? Wasn't the truth that he had been too comfortable in St Andrews? There was the appeal of a small university compared to Edinburgh and Glasgow; meeting colleagues in the wynds and going for coffees; dining at their elegant houses with their established gardens. He should have been bolder and looked across the Atlantic, to the Ivy League universities. If Grace Armstrong could get a post at Harvard, why couldn't he? But he hadn't been as industrious and adventurous as she was. She had built a career on the Bloomsbury Set of artists: he could have done the same with Hellenistic sculpture – except that the subject wasn't as fashionable as libertine Bloomsbury. Why didn't he finish his study years ago? When he looked back he found it difficult to answer this question in a way that wasn't an excuse. He had had plenty of time, not having a particularly heavy teaching load, and no other research interest. He must have spent too long thinking about the book, rather than getting down to writing it. He had done most of the research, after all, and, at least in the early years, had the field to himself. Vivien had achieved much more than he had. There were half a dozen stained glass windows by her in various locations in Scotland to admire.

Mackilligin was now learning a late lesson about life. At his age we look back and want to select the most fulfilling and happier parts, and to discard the rest. But life has to be appraised as a whole, with all its flaws, like a painting. There are coarse textures, areas of the broad canvas where the light is flawed, and there are the mistakes that cannot be covered up, however much paint one applies. The art historian realised now that seducing one of his students had been a gross act of betrayal, not only of her, but of himself, and that it had tainted his veneration for the purity of Hellenistic statuary. It was arrogance and vanity to think that he could go back in time and find happiness and fulfilment in a person of a younger generation. It was also predatory, and he was duly ashamed.

Once home from his walk by the sea he began to prepare lunch, which Rebecca came down for, but went back upstairs immediately after she had eaten. She was spending most of her time in the studio, except when she walked along the Scores to St James's Catholic Church, where she lit a candle daily on the rack for her dead infant and sat in the front pew, including her husband as well in her prayers. She found comfort in the admission that she was as much to blame as he was for the sin of their sexually charged affair and for the conception that had led to tragic loss. But out of it had come early maturity and a loving relationship with her mother, after the years of dislike and recrimination. When she rose from her penance she touched the feet of the wooden Madonna standing above the flaming tiers of candles, as if that contact would give her inspiration for her stained glass creation.

'I need to buy more glass,' she informed her husband, and he gave her his already laden credit card to use over the phone.

The sheets arrived by courier and she carried them carefully up the stairs, as if it were a child in her arms. Sometimes, as he passed the shut door, he fancied he could hear the rasp of her glass cutter, but it might have been a memory of a dead hand guiding it. Winter brought gales, and he lay trembling in bed, not at the fury of the wind, but at the realisation that he couldn't recall the names of students he had taught the previous year. Yet ask him about a class list of twenty years ago and he could probably give fifty per cent of the names.

When he took his green bags to the supermarket, he returned with items missing, even though he had made a list. 'Why have you bought sausages, which we never eat?' Rebecca wanted to know, but he couldn't bring himself to confess that his memory was going, and that he found himself in shops which weren't on his list, standing at counters, trying to explain what he wanted to bewildered assistants.

He had gone to the dispensing machine in the wall of the bank to draw cash, but couldn't remember his PIN number. He tried three separate combinations, and then went into the bank. They had machines on the counter now which required the customer to insert his card and key in his number. The art historian explained to the assistant that he had forgotten his PIN number. She was suspicious and asked him for identification. It was humiliating, being treated like a person trying to draw money from someone else's account, and he had to stand for five minutes, causing a queue until another member of the bank's staff appeared and took him into a small bare room like a cell.

'You've forgotten your PIN number, Professor Mackilligin?'

'I'm sorry, but I have.'

'Do you think you'll be able to remember it in the future?'

'I'll try, but I can't guarantee that I will.'

'Are you on some kind of medication?'

'No, but my memory seems to be going.'

'Have you been to your doctor?'

'Not yet.'

'I think you should,' the young woman advised, concerned. 'I notice that you have a joint account with your wife. Can't you get her to withdraw cash when you need it on her PIN number?'

'I don't want her to know about what's happening to my memory.'

'You need to go to your doctor, professor. Obviously

every time you need cash we can't go through a procedure of identification, especially when it's a busy bank. I'll go and get you the two hundred pounds you were trying to withdraw.'

He didn't tell Rebecca about what had happened at the bank. But he made an appointment with Dr Anderson, who was sympathetic and asked his patient several questions about himself from his records which he had on his screen. He knew his date of birth, but forgot that his middle name was Gordon, and he couldn't remember the name of the current Prime Minister.

'I'll send you for tests.'

He told Rebecca that he was going across to Dundee to check something in the university library there. He used his senior pass on the bus, and at the clinic he was given tests involving shapes – the same kind of tests he recalled when he had sat his Qualifying examination in primary school.

'It doesn't look good, does it?' he said to the psychologist.

'You've made a few basic mistakes. We need to investigate this further. I'll write to Dr Anderson.'

His GP sent him back to Dundee, for a scan, and when the consultant showed him the result on the screen, he pointed out the areas of damage to his brain.

'How long have I got before my memory goes?' he asked fearfully.

'That's impossible to say, professor. It won't disappear dramatically overnight, but it will gradually get worse, over months or even years. I'll send my report to Dr Anderson this week, and you should make an appointment with him for next week.'

When he went to see Anderson the scan of his brain was up on the screen of his computer in front of him.

'Have you discussed the situation with your wife?'

'Not yet.'

'You should do so as soon as possible, professor. She needs to know so that you can both look at your domestic arrangements.'

'I'll tell her soon,' he promised.

'If it makes it any easier we can arrange a consultation here with both of you and I can tell her and explain the implications.'

'Thank you, doctor, but it's my place to tell her.'

'We can give you a lot of support from here when you begin to experience difficulties,' Anderson reassured him. 'Come and see me in a month – earlier if you have problems.'

But he didn't tell Rebecca about the diagnosis. It was too early after the loss of their child to burden her with more grief and besides, she was deep into a creative period with her stained glass work, and he didn't want to disrupt it. Some nights he left his bed and went to the corner where the cot had stood, to check on the dead, because time was playing cruel tricks on him.

'Is this a joke, Alan?' Rebecca challenged him when he served on her plate a fish, still with its head and skin.

'It's the way they used to eat them,' he tried to lie his way out of his shame.

She didn't notice his difficulties and mistakes, she was so preoccupied with her work. She had now started to assemble the lead and glass, locking in the lead borders, opening up the channel in the metal with the lathekin. She was ready to insert the first piece of glass into the corner junction, fitting it into the lead channels, then tapping it lightly with the small block of wood. She was measuring the next lead when he called her down to lunch.

'I don't see you working on your book,' she commented, having complained that the soup was stone-cold. (He had forgotten to switch on the gas under the pot).

'I've abandoned it.'

'Abandoned it? Why?' she asked, tearing the hunk of bread in two.

'Because it wasn't working out. I found that I couldn't reconstruct it.'

But he didn't tell her that it was a jumble of incomprehensible words which he had erased, the hard drive pristine again, the laptop shelved.

'That's a pity.' She started to giggle. 'Why have you got on two different shoes? You're not getting eccentric, are you, like Professor Murchison?'

The Biblical scholar was a well-kent sight in St Andrews, wandering the streets and wynds, talking to himself and pulling anguished faces as he debated a passage in the New Testament with himself. Mackilligin had seen him on a wet day, wearing a woman's plastic rain-mate, the manuscript of an impenetrable book on the Gospel of Mark in the carrier bag with the bread and cheese he ate on a bench in Market Street, his feet without socks.

Rebecca went back upstairs, leaving him to wash up. It

took him a long time, handling the dishes carefully because there had been a lot of breakages of late. Of the Spode dinner service Vivien and he had received from her parents, only about half remained, and his late wife had certainly broken none of it. He couldn't replace the pieces because they were out of production.

Some evenings when Rebecca was working upstairs he sat down and made a conscious effort to remember what he had been doing that day. He tried to write out a running order, beginning with breakfast, but he had forgotten where he had gone when he went out. Did he go to the university library, to look up a reference? Not likely, since he had abandoned his Hellenistic book and besides, he had difficulty getting round the art section, though six months ago he could have gone blind-folded between the shelves and put his hand on the appropriate classical sculpture section. Now he couldn't recall the names of the statues he had written about. Had he gone shopping? He must have had, because he was the sole provider of food. Which shops had he been in? Surely Tesco. If so, what had he bought? What they had had for supper. But what had that been? Fish or meat?

He knew that he shouldn't subject himself to these reconstructions because they only caused him terror at the thought that nothing new was entering his memory now. But it was getting even more sinister than that. It was as if his memory were being eaten away, backwards, so that as he lived another week, he lost another month. He was now having difficulty remembering the details of his first meeting with Rebecca. Where had it been, in the garden of St Mary's, or in St Salvator's?

He went to sit in the Chapel, to see if he could connect, but as his lucidity faded his terror increased. It seemed to him that the high-backed uncomfortable pews were peopled by professors who had served the university down the centuries, but whose names, as his would be, had been forgotten, their scientific researches, and their literary endeavours superseded and neglected, their dusty tomes stacked in the basement of the library behind a steel grille, accessed by a swipe-card and by a wheel turned to open up the bays on rails.

In another rare interlude of philosophical lucidity Mackilligin had another thought: scholars who wrote about the glories of classical art, or writers of the status of Tolstoy ended up knowing as much – or as little – about the purpose of life as the person who made their shoes. Poets and philosophers had insights into the process of living, but that was not the same as understanding why we are here, and where we are going – if anywhere. It was hidden, like the pudenda of the Aphrodite of Cnidus under her palm.

He was going to have to tell Rebecca very soon about his deteriorating condition because, when she finished the design she was working on, she was going to notice it. Sometimes he was almost caught out in conversations. She said to him:

'You remember that time when mummy came to see us to make it up?'

'When was that?'

'Come on, you must remember. She took us to the fish restaurant along the Scores.'

'I've never eaten in that restaurant,' he said.

'I know what you're trying to do – you're making out that mummy never made an apology to you by claiming that you can't remember her taking us both for a meal. I regard that as an insult to myself as well as to her. OK, she failed me as a mother, but at least she came to see us after the death of Felicity.'

'Who was Felicity?'

'You know what I think, Alan – you're drinking in secret. This isn't the first time recently that I've noticed you behaving like this. You must have drunk a lot to have forgotten your daughter's name.'

He wanted to tell her about his advancing dementia, but couldn't find the courage, so he said: 'I do take the odd glass of whisky from time to time when I'm feeling depressed.'

'More like a whole bottle. You're taking advantage of the fact that I'm working most of the time upstairs and I don't see what you're bringing in in the way of drink. If you're not careful you're going to become an alcoholic, and I won't put up with that.'

'I'll stop,' he promised. 'It's thinking about Felicity that upsets me.'

But as soon as he said the name he had forgotten who she was. Rebecca went upstairs to her design and he was left weeping over the disintegration of his mind.

Chapter 20

'I've finished,' Rebecca announced, and for the first time in weeks allowed her husband into the studio to show him the design.

It was of a naked child with outstretched arms running through a meadow.

'It's wonderful,' he told her. It was as if he could smell the blue and yellow flowers cut so carefully out of glass. 'How did you manage to get the blades of grass to bend so beautifully?'

'I've been well trained by Jessica Rae, and your wife had such quality tools.'

'We need to go out to celebrate,' he told her. 'Where would you like to go?'

'The Seafood Restaurant on the Scores. Will you book a table?'

But he had difficulty looking up the phone book, so he asked her to do it while he got dressed. He was also having problems knotting a tie now. He watched his arms in the mirror, but they didn't seem to belong to him any more, so he decided to go in an open-necked shirt, though it had never been his outdoor style. This time he checked carefully to see that he was wearing two shoes the same. It was a beautiful evening and the low sun was shining through the plate glass walls on to their table, making the cutlery ripple like fire. He made it easier for himself by ordering the first dish on the menu. When the waiter brought the wine list he told him to make the choice and when the bottle arrived, chilled in its bucket, they toasted her success by clinking glasses.

'I've something to tell you, Alan.'

He was waiting to hear that she had sold her stained glass design.

'I've met someone else.'

He sat in silence, as if he hadn't heard, but he had taken it in.

'I'm so sorry to have to tell you like this, but there's never a good time for such a disclosure.'

She reached across the table to cover his hand. He should say: *and I have something to tell you – something I should have told you months ago. I have Early Onset Alzheimer's.* Instead he asked: 'is it someone I know?'

'I don't think so. He just joined the School of English a year ago. His name is Roger Hempleton and he's a brilliant scholar, an international authority on Faulkner, with a prize-winning book to his credit, though he's only twenty nine.'

Mackilligin didn't say: *I'm immensely relieved, because now I don't have to tell you about my condition. You have no responsibilities towards me and can go and make a new and much more fulfilling life for yourself.* Instead he said: 'I suppose you're going to move in with him.'

'Yes.'

'And you'll want a divorce.'

'I'm so sorry, Alan.'

He held up a hand. 'You're still my wife and are entitled to half of what we have – including the house.'

She shook her head emphatically. 'Roger and I have

discussed this, Alan, and I don't want a penny from you. I'm confident I can make money out of commissions, and Roger's in the running for a Fellowship in Oxford. If he gets it we'll leave St Andrews and not embarrass you.'

Mackilligin had one of these rare moments of clarity which are sometimes granted to dementia sufferers. As he listened to his wife's optimistic plans for a new beginning with her lover, he realised that he had had a privileged life compared to what hers would be. He had come of age in the carefree vibrant 1960s, when generous grants had funded his education, and he had had money in the bank instead of debts when he left university. He had known the long-term stability of faithful love, a marriage not threatened by infidelity, or destroyed by divorce, and he had had the freedom from a reasonable teaching timetable to pursue his researches. He had travelled extensively to elite universities, giving lectures and seminars, without having to think about the effect aeroplanes were having on the environment, and he had a good pension. But the young woman sitting opposite him wouldn't have the same privileges. The onset of global warming would force changes in her lifestyle. Money would become tighter, and buying a plane ticket would become an act of conscience. She would find it difficult to get stained glass commissions in an age of austerity, and her lover at Oxford would have an increasingly heavy teaching burden. And if they had children, the world for them would be a bleaker, more problematic place.

But the moment of clarity was gone, and when the main

course arrived, Mackilligin's concern was: which cutlery to use?

The following day she packed her belongings.

'I'd like to take your wife's stained glass tools,' she told him.

'No,' he said firmly. 'They belong here.'

She didn't make an issue out of it, though nobody else would use them. She made several trips with her possessions to the abode of her lover, an atmospheric flat in a wynd. He was lecturing, but she had the key she had been using for months.

Mackilligin had enough alertness left to remind her, as she was leaving their home for the last time: 'You've forgotten your stained glass panel.'

'It's a present for you, to remind you of Felicity.'

But he still couldn't recall who Felicity was, and put the panel in a cupboard. He expected the house to be lonely, but it wasn't. He took up mugs of coffee, thinking that Vivien was working in her studio, and during the night he reached out, believing that he could feel her presence.

In St Salvator's Chapel the porter, new to the staff, noticed an elderly man sitting in one of the high-backed pews reserved for staff. He went down the aisle and told him gently that he was locking up for the night.

'I'm waiting to hear her play,' the old man protested.

'Who, sir?'

'Rebecca. She'll be coming in any minute to practise.'

'Rebecca?' the porter queried.

'She's a student in theology and classics.'

'I don't know her, sir, and I know the names of the students who are authorised to play the organ.'

'She's a very fine player, particularly of Bach.'

'I don't think she can be coming this evening, sir.'

'Perhaps she's been delayed.'

The porter took the elderly man's arm and helped him down the aisle slowly, because he was unsteady on his feet.

'Where do you live, sir?'

'I can't remember the address, but it's just round the corner.'

'Will you manage, sir?' the porter asked as he helped him through the cloisters.

'I'm fine, thank you. I'll come back tomorrow evening, to hear Rebecca play. She puts such feeling into Bach, it would make you weep.'

When he went into the porters' lodge under the Hebdomadar's Room he told his colleague about the stranger sitting in the Chapel.

'That's Professor Mackilligin. He's in there most evenings, waiting for some student called Rebecca to play the organ. He's lost his mind, though he can't be seventy.'

'And when I see him again?' the new porter asked.

'Be gentle with him. He's a poor soul.'

Dr Anderson stopped him in the street.

'How are you, professor? You look well and remarkably happy.'

'I'm very happy, Doctor. Vivien and I are going to Iona next week. I'm going to ask her parents if I may marry her. She's a wonderful person.'

There were days of serenity, days of anguish; days when he became lost in the wynds he had known so well; lost too in the labyrinth of his mind.

Two years later, accompanying her husband back to St Andrews where he was delivering a lecture, Rebecca and he were walking along the Scores. She was gloriously happy in her new circumstances, and had won a major commission for a stained glass window in Oxfordshire on which she would start after the baby was born in two months' time. She looked up to the nursing home and saw the face of the Hellenistic statuary expert at a window in the nursing home. She waved but there was no recognition, as if he had turned to stone.